I0554197

"Time to Break the Barrier"

Written By

Sharnel Williams

Alma Collins Thomas

Tukisha M. Know

Shar-Shey Publishing Company, LLC

P.O. Box 841

Tobyhanna, PA 18466

(973) 348-5067

www.sharsheypublishingcompany.com

sspublishingcompany@gmail.com

ISBN-13: 978-0997266832

ISBN- 10: 099726683X

Editor: ATW Editing

Cover Design: Thaiala Gardner

This book was printed in the United States of America.

Sick & Tired

By

Sharnel Williams

Sharnel Williams

I'm a wife, mother, author, radio host, entrepreneur and grandmother.

Born and raised in Newark, NJ. I have two children, one living and one that passed away from leukemia in 2005.

I started my own company in 2016, called Shar-Shey Publishing Company, LLC. I have so much to give to others. I'm on a mission to grow my company and turn my first book into a movie. I want to thank all of my supporters.

www.authorsharnel.com

www.sharsheypublishingcompany.com

sharnelwilliams@ymail.com

Acknowledgement

I want to thank God, first and foremost.

I want to thank my husband (Kevin), son (Kevin) and grandson (Noah).

I'm thanking my family and friends, who believe in me.

I'm shouting out all my supporters, who purchase and read all my books.

I appreciate the love.

I want to thank Alma Collins Thomas and Tukisha M. Knox for agreeing to write this anthology.

Trust in Believe you can accomplish your Dreams, if you Believe.

Jennifer "Myami" Lucas met Howard "Howie" Johnson at an event in the park one summer day. Myami and her friends walked by a group of men.

Howie shouted out, "Hey girl in the purple tank top!"

Myami looked back and continued walking. Howie and his friends started following them.

He continued screaming out, "Hey girl in the purple tank top." As his voice got stronger and frustrated, he yelled out, "You are not all that," and turned around and headed back to the spot they were originally at.

A couple of hours later, Myami and her friends started walking back toward the guys. Howie spotted them and ran up to Myami.

"Hello," he spoke.

Myami replied hello.

"What's your name?"

"Myami."

"Nice name and you have a pretty smile."

She laughed and said, "Thank you."

Howie's friends started calling him. "Come on Howie! Come on Howie!"

He looked back and waved his hand. He asked her for her number, but she said, "No, give me yours."

He laughed as she handed him her cell phone and he put his number in the phone. When he was done, he turned around, running to catch up with his friends.

Myami looked back and yelled, "What's your name?"

He screamed out, "HOWIE".

"He's kind of cute," she whispered to her friends. They all started laughing and walking down the block. Once everyone was near their home, each of the girls began walking toward their respective homes.

Myami walked into her house.

"Jenni, is that you?" her mother yelled.

"Yeah, Mom!" she replied. As she walked in the kitchen, she asked her mom, "What you cooking?"

"A little of this and a little of that."

Myami started laughing.

"Get ready for dinner. Your father will be home in a minute."

Myami walked up the stairs and heard her phone beeping. She reached in her pocket for her phone to see who was texting her. It was her friend Amenda.

Amenda: Hey Myami! I've been thinking about you since we left the festival. What are you doing?

Myami: I'm washing up for dinner. What are you doing?

Amenda: Nothing. Did you call that guy yet?

Myami: "Giggles"

Amenda: What's so funny?

Myami: Nothing.

Amenda: Well did you?

Myami: No!

Amenda: I will talk to you tomorrow, goodnight.

Myami put her phone on the bed and went to the bathroom. Once she came out, she texted Howie.

Myami: Hey, Howie.

Howie: Hello, Myami.

Myami: What are you doing?

Howie: Nothing. What are you doing?

Myami: Nothing. I'm about to eat in a few.

Howie: You cooking?

Myami: No, my mom does all the cooking

Howie: Are you seeing anyone?

Myami: Are you seeing anyone?

Howie: No.

Myami: Can we finish this conversation later? It's time for dinner. Next time I will call you, no texting.

Howie: LOL. I will be waiting for your call or maybe I'll call you.

Myami's mother called her downstairs to eat.

"I'm coming, Mom." She had a smile on her face as she ran down the stairs.

"Are you alright?" her mom asked.

"Yes, I'm fine now."

Her mom looked at her and shook her head. Her father was sitting at the table, just looking at Myami. "Hey, baby girl".

"Hey, Dad. How was your day?"

"Long and tired."

Myami smiled at her father's stare, then sat down at the kitchen table. Myami's phone started ringing. She jumped up to run upstairs.

Her father said, "No you don't. Girl, if you don't sit down and eat your food."

Myami sat down as she was told and grabbed a biscuit. She started thinking about Howie. She had finished eating and excused herself from the table. She went up into her bedroom, flopped across the bed, and looked at her phone to see who had called her. It was a missed call from one of her friends, Lisa. She dialed the number back.

"What's up?" Miami said.

"Did you speak to that guy?" Lisa asked.

"What guy?" Myami replied.

"The guy from the festival."

"Oh, Howie! Yes, I texted him earlier."

Her friend was so excited for her. She yelled through the phone. "What did he say?"

"Nothing really." Myami responded.

"Nothing really?"

"Yes, nothing really," Myami told her friend. "He's supposed to call me later."

They both started laughing and hung up the phone. Myami walked over to her desk and turned on her laptop.

"You want some dessert?" asked her mom as she walked into Myami's room.

"Not now, maybe later," Myami answered.

"Don't stay up too late. We have to go out tomorrow."

"Where?"

"You will find out tomorrow. Good night!"

Myami turned on Spotify and put in her wireless ear plugs. She walked over to her bed and lay across it listening to her playlist. Next thing she knew, her mom was knocking on her bedroom door at 8:00am in the morning. Myami had fallen asleep listening to her music last night.

"Come in."

Her mom opened the door and walked in. "You have to get up now and get ready. Why do you have on your clothes from yesterday?"

Myami replied, "I must have fallen asleep."

"Well let's go. Get up."

Myami turned her head, grabbed her pillow, and covered her face.

"Get Up! We're going to be late," her mom yelled to her.

Myami slowly turned around and asked her mom, "Do I really have to go with you? Why do you need me to go?"

"Just get up and get dressed. I'm not telling you again."

Myami jumped out of bed. "Alright, I'm up. Are you happy now?" She went into the bathroom and turned on the shower. As she pushed the shower curtain back and climbed in the shower, she heard a phone ringing. She turned off the water to make sure it was her cell phone that was ringing that early in the morning. She turned the water back on and started washing up. She was thinking about her phone. She was wondering who was calling her so early in the morning because it was the summer and school was out. She stepped out of the shower onto the rug and grabbed the towel off the hook. She dried off then wrapped the towel around her body and walked to her room. She headed over to her phone and checked the number. It was a private number, so she threw her phone on the bed. She walked over to her closet and pulled out her banana colored maxi dress.

Her mom walked back into her room. "Are you wearing that?"

'Yes, I am."

"Well okay, just come on."

Myami had just graduated and her mom wanted to surprise her with a gift she would never forget. Once dressed, Myami walked into the living room where her mother was waiting for her. They went out the door and got into the car. After a short drive, they pulled up in front of a car lot.

"Mom, does your car have to be worked on or something?" Myami asked, concerned about her mother.

"No, just be quiet and follow me."

They walked into the office and Myami's mother asked for Salesman Tommy. Another salesman paged him for her. Tommy walked from the back.

"Hello, Ms. Lucas. How have you been?"

"Fine and you?

"This must be Jennifer." He reached out to shake her hand.

"You can call me Myami."

"Hello, Myami, and nice to meet you."

"Nice to meet you too, Tom." Myami walked over by her mother and asked, "Why are we here and how do you know Tom?"

"His name is Tommy, not Tom," her mother stated.

"Well he didn't correct me. I'm sure his friends call him Tom."

"Just come over here, girl."

9

They sat at Tommy's desk.

"You act like you don't want to be here," Tommy said to Myami

"I don't." Myami smirked.

"Hopefully that will change." He asked Myami for her driver's license.

"Why you need my DL?"

"Girl, give him your license," stated her mom.

"What's going on?" Myami questioned.

"I can show you better than I can tell you," Tommy stated before he got out of his chair and told them to follow him. They walked through two open doors as they headed toward the back of the company.

"Are you buying me a car?" she asked her mother with a questioning look on her face.

Her mom just smiled and said, "Congratulations!"

Myami was so excited as she hugged and kissed her mom. She was overwhelmed with excitement. They walked out to the parking area. There it was—a shiny, two-door, black 2015 Nissan Altima. She jumped up and down.

"Mom, how did you know this was the kind of car I wanted?"

"I heard you talking about it on the phone a couple of months ago."

Myami started laughing and hugged her mom again. "I love you, Mom."

"I love you too."

Myami opened the car door and got in. She had a smile so huge on her face. Myami called one of her friends to tell her the news. After she hung up her cell phone, her mother said, "We have to talk about the rules first, Myami."

"Rules?"

"There will be no drinking and driving, no letting your friends drive or borrow the car, and you must follow the speed limit. If you fail to abide by these rules, I will take your car from you.

"Mom..."

"Please don't try me." Then she walked away.

"Are you getting the car, Ms. Lucas?" the salesman inquired.

"Yes."

"Are you sure?"

"Finish the paperwork," her mother stated with finality. "Oh, Jennifer, you have to get a job too."

Myami looked at her mom. "A job?"

"Yes J-O-B."

"If I was going to college would I have to get a job and pay for this car?"

"No. Since you want to take a year off and wait to go to college, you will have to get a job to help pay your bills."

"My bills?"

"Yes, your bills. You have a cell phone and now you have a car note with car insurance."

Myami held her head down.

"I will help you, but I can't do it all by myself. It's only right. We are not rich."

"The paperwork is complete. I just need your signature," Tommy said after walking back to the car where Myami and her mother were talking.

"My signature?"

"Yes!"

"The car is going in my name?"

Tommy and her mother answered at the same time.
"Yes."

"So, don't mess your credit up." Her mother smirked with a serious face.

Everything was good. They drove off the lot. Myami followed her mother home. They pulled up in front of the house. Myami looked at all the cars parked in the driveway. She started thinking, 'What's going on?' She thought something happened to her dad. She opened her car door and called out to her mom.

"Mom! Mom!"

"What, girl?"

"Is everything okay?"

"Yes, girl. Now go in the house."

Myami opened the door and everyone screamed, "Congratulations." She looked at her mom and dad and started crying. They had given her a Graduation Party. She was so happy. She looked around the house and saw all her friends and family. She pulled one of her friends' arms and said, "Everyone look!" She took them outside to see the car. They all crowded around the vehicle and said it was nice. Some pulled out their phones to take pictures with the car. Everyone went back into the house and started eating and dancing. Myami was so happy, she still couldn't believe her parents had surprised her with a brand-new car. She went to her bedroom and called Howie.

As soon as Howie picked up his phone he asked, "What's going on?"

"My parents just bought me a new car and they're throwing me a party!"

"When?"

"Now. Come over for a while."

"Are you for real?"

"I wouldn't be asking if I wasn't for real." He asked her for her address before saying he'd be right over. They hung up the phone and she headed back downstairs.

"I invited a friend over to the party. I hope it's okay," she whispered in her mother's ear.

"Sure, it's your day."

Myami kept walking over by the window and looking out of it. No sign of Howie. She started getting nervous as she asked herself if he was coming. She ran upstairs to use the bathroom and thought about calling him. She shook her head no and laid her phone on the sink. As she looked in the mirror at herself, she saw that her hair was a little messy, grabbed the brush and started brushing her hair up into a pony tail. The music was so loud she could barely hear. Her mother started calling her. She yelled downstairs, "Here I come!"

She walked down the stairs and there was Howie. He looked up at her with a huge smile on his face. She looked down at him with a huge smile on her face.

"Who is this?" her dad asked.

With the smile still on her face, she replied, "This is Howie. I met him at the festival last week."

Her dad gave him a handshake and her mother spoke with a soft voice. She started walking him around and introducing him to everyone at the party. She repeated over and over, "he is not my boyfriend." Howie had a grin on his face that would steal any girl's heart.

"Let's get to know Howie. Turn the music off," Myami suggested.

"How old are you?" her mother asked.

"Eighteen," Howie answered, glad it was an easy question.

"What grade are you in?" her dad inquired.

"I graduated last year and I'm going to community college this year."

"Why are you giving him the twenty questions?" Myami asked her parents.

"Does anyone else have any questions?" Myami screamed out. "We are just friends."

"You want to dance?" Howie asked Myami.

"Yes."

Everyone in attendance was having a great time. The party started winding down and everyone started saying their good-byes. After the house was empty, Myami and Howie went to sit on the porch. They found out they had a lot in common with one another. Myami wanted to go to the movies, but she didn't know how to ask Howie. She finally got the nerve. "It's still early. Do you want to go see a movie?"

"Sure."

Myami took out her phone to google the movies that were playing. They both agreed on one flick. She got up and walked into her house. She called her mom and her mom said to come in the kitchen.

"I'm going out for a while."

"Where?" her mother questioned.

"Howie and I are going to the movies."

"Don't forget you have a curfew."

"I know. 11:00 pm."

"And don't turn off your phone," her father interjected.

Myami gave her parents a kiss and started laughing.

"Drive safe," her mother reminded her.

———————

After watching the movie, Myami asked Howie a question. "Where do you live so I can take you home?"

"I drove to your house. I don't need a ride."

"Excuse me, I didn't know you had a car."

"I don't. It's my mother's car," he said.

"Oh okay."

"Why are you looking at me like that?"

"Like what?" Myami asked.

"Nothing."

Myami pulled up in front of his mom's car and said, "Nice car."

Howie got out of the car. "I will call you in a few."

After parking her car, Myami got out, walked into her house, and closed the door.

"Jenni! Jenni! Is that you?" her mom yelled out.

"Yes, Mom."

"How was your date?"

Myami starting laughing. "Date? I told you we are just friends."

"He's a handsome boy," her mother stated.

Myami didn't pay that any mind as she walked to her room to get ready for bed.

———————

The summer was almost over, which meant it was time for Howie to go to college and time for Myami to find a job. She'd been on three interviews, but not one had called yet. She would go out every day to buy the newspaper and search for possible jobs. One day she opened the newspaper and saw they were having a job fair in her old school gym. She went into the kitchen to tell her mother about the job fair.

After informing her mother of what she found, she immediately had a thought. "It's tomorrow and I don't have anything to wear."

"Find something. You have a closet full of clothes."

Myami woke up at 8:00am and realized she had forgotten to set her alarm. She jumped up and ran into the bathroom. She took a birdbath and put on her clothes. She grabbed her purse and ran downstairs. "Mother! What happened? You didn't wake me up."

"I didn't know I was supposed to wake you up. You have an alarm clock."

"The job fair started at 8:00 this morning."

Her mom replied, "You never told me what time it started."

Myami ran out of the house and jumped into her car. She was so nervous. She really wanted a job now. She was surprised that she had been thinking about a job lately; she had never thought about it until her mother mentioned it. She pulled up into the school parking lot and was amazed by the turnout. There were so many people there, including one of her old teachers with her son. She walked over and gave her a hug. She looked across the gym and saw Howie and his friends. It surprised her to see him. She thought he was going to college. Howie walked over to where Myami was standing.

He was the first to speak. "What's up? I didn't know you was looking for a job."

"And I didn't know you was looking for a job."

"I need a part time job."

"What about college?"

"Yes, I'm going to do that too. What about you?"

"My mom told me I need one to help her pay for this car I will be driving." They both laughed and walked out of the gym into the hallway.

"I thought I would never step back into this school."

"Me neither. You are going to be so busy, you won't have time for a personal life."

"Are you talking about us spending time together?"

"No," Myami answered with her face frowned up.

They walked to the front door and headed towards Myami's car.

"Let's hang out later." She got in her car, beeped the horn and drove off.

———————

Myami's mom was looking out of the window and saw Myami pulling up. She went to open the door for her. She gave her mom a kiss on the cheek as soon as she walked in the house.

"What are you doing?" Myami asked her mother.

"I was checking my e-mail until I saw you pull up. How was the job fair?"

"It was great and I saw one of my old teachers. Guess who else was there?"

"Girl, just tell me. This is not a guessing game."

Myami started laughing and said, "Howie."

"Howie? Oh Howie! What, he met you there?"

"No," Myami answered. "He is looking for a part time job."

"Really?"

"Yes, Mom. He really has everything planned out while he's in college."

"That's great. He's on the right track."

"I really want one of the employers to call me. You were right, Mom. I need a job and money in my pocket." Myami was so excited about getting a job. She went upstairs to write down some goals for her life. She grabbed a pen and paper. She titled the top page of the paper and wrote, "Myami's Goals."

1-Finish College

2-Get a good job

3-Get married

4-Get a house

5-Start a family

In between I would like to start my own clothing design business. I learned a lot today about the importance of planning your future.

After writing down her goals, she hung the paper on her mirror. Her phone rang. It was Howie.

"What's up, Howie?" Myami answered.

"Nothing. What are we doing tonight?"

"Tonight?" Myami asked with a puzzled look on her face.

"Yes, didn't you say we were going to see one another later?"

"Oh yeah. What do you want to do?"

"Just chill. Do you want to come over to my house and watch some Netflix and eat some popcorn?"

Myami paused for a minute.

"Hello, are you still here?" Howie asked when she was silent for too long.

Coming out of her thoughts, Myami answered him. "Yes I am."

"What's up, Myami? Are you coming over?"

"Yes, give me like an hour." After she hung up the phone, she started thinking out loud. "Should I go over to his house?" she asked as she looked in the mirror talking to herself. "I know he just probably wants sex and I'm not ready for that." She started getting nervous. She had never been to a boy's house before. She thought about calling him back and telling him her mother wouldn't let her out. Then she said to herself, "He knows my curfew is at 11:00 pm."

She stood straight up and grabbed her hair into a pony tail. As she walked down the stairs, she yelled to her mom, "I'll be back in a few. Going out for a while."

Her mom came out of the family room. "Where are you going?"

"With a couple of my friends for a while. They want to go get some ice cream." She gave her mom a kiss and walked out the front door. She couldn't believe she had just lied to her mother. She had never lied to her mom a day in her life. She held her head up toward the sky and asked God to forgive her.

She pulled up in front of Howie's apartment building. She texted him and told him to come downstairs. She started looking around. There were a lot of people in front of the building. To be honest, she was a little scared to get out of the car. This was a totally different neighborhood from where she lived and grew up. She popped the locks as she saw Howie walking toward the car. He opened the door and sat in the front seat.

"What's wrong?"

"Nothing," she said nervously. She had the neighborhood on her mind. She kept looking around and over her shoulder.

"Are you sure you are alright?"

"Yes, I'm fine. Why you keep asking me that?"

"Forget about it. Let's go upstairs."

They got out of the car and she hit the button for her alarm. As Myami got closer to the steps, she grabbed her pocketbook tighter. Howie pushed the button for the elevator.

"I don't do elevators," Myami stated.

Howie started laughing. "Well, I do. Girl, I live on the 8th floor. There's no way I'm walking."

"The 8th floor? What the hell? I didn't know you lived in an apartment building."

"Where you thought I lived?"

"In a house."

"I was born and raised in the projects!"

Once they reached his apartment, he introduced Myami to his little sister and brother, then grabbed her hand and walked to his bedroom. He opened the door and she walked in.

"Why are there two beds?" Myami asked.

"Me and my little brother share a room."

Myami walked over and sat in the chair and Howie went to make some popcorn. He entered the room with a bowl of popcorn before closing and locking the door.

"You alright?" he inquired. Myami nodded her head up and down. "What type of movies do you like?"

"It doesn't matter. I'll watch what you watch."

As he was scrolling across the TV screen, Myami yelled, "Turn back."

"For what?"

She saw a movie called "Pretty in Pink" that was one of her favorite movies. She hadn't seen it in a while. "Have you ever seen this movie?"

"No."

"Well, there's a first time for everything." He clapped his hands and the lights went off. He sat in the chair right next to Myami. She scooted over a little to make room for him.

"This is an old movie. What's it about?"

"It's a romance/love story."

"A love story?"

"Yes," Myami said. "You can turn it if you want to."

"No, let's watch it," Howie said to her

———————

It was getting close to Myami's curfew and she had to get ready to head home.

27

"How did you like the movie?" Myami questioned Howie.

"It was a good movie, if you believe in love."

She shook her head. "You don't believe in love?"

"I haven't met the right girl yet."

Myami smiled before pulling his arm. "Walk me to my car?"

He jumped up. "Let's go!"

When they made it to her car, she got in and Howie sat in the passenger seat.

"Turn the music on."

She kept looking at the clock. She didn't want to be late for her curfew. She already felt guilty for lying to her mother earlier. She explained to Howie about her curfew and told him she would call him once she got home. He gave her a kiss on the cheek and got out of the car. She drove off hoping she would make her curfew on time.

———————

Her mom was looking out the window and saw her driving up. She pulled the curtain over and pretended like she was reading a book. Myami opened the front door and saw the reading light on in the dining room.

"Mom, are you in the dining room?" she called out.

"I'm reading," her mother answered.

Myami headed up the stairs and her mom called out to her. "Wait a minute. How was your night?"

"It was alright. I'm tired. I'm going to bed."

She texted Howie to let him know she was home.

Howie texted back: *Call me.*

She dialed his number and his phone was ringing. He picked up.

"I wanted to hear your voice," he stated as soon as he answered the phone.

"Hear my voice?"

"Yes, now I can go to sleep. Good night!"

————————

In the morning, Myami smelled food coming from downstairs. She jumped out of bed and went into the bathroom to take care of her hygiene. She yelled down the stairs, "Make enough for me." She heard her phone beep and grabbed it to see who was texting her. Months had gone by and she and Howie were officially girlfriend and boyfriend. Howie started spending more time at her house. Her parents were getting close to him, especially her father. He thought he was going to make something out of his life and he was good for his daughter.

They started working together at a warehouse in the downtown area. At first it was nice. They were together every day almost every minute. The only time they were apart was when Howie was in school. Howie started working more hours at work. It started to interfere with his schoolwork. Myami started doing his homework for him and that gave him more time to get plenty of hours. He wanted to buy a car and that was the only thing he was focusing on at the time. Myami was getting tired of doing his homework, but she didn't know how to tell him. So she went to vent to her mother. She told her mother what was going on.

Her mother couldn't believe Myami had been doing his homework all that time so he could work more hours to buy a car. She shook her head. "Myami, you have to stop doing his work for him."

"I don't want to hurt his feelings and I don't want him to be mad at me."

Her mom just walked away huffing and puffing.

Myami repeatedly asked her mother, "What am I supposed to do? I love him."

"Do the right thing."

Myami started walking up the stairs to her room. She turned on the TV and turned the volume down low. She knew around this time, Howie was in school. She really didn't want to tell him, but she was tired of doing his homework. She lay across the bed and fell asleep. A couple of hours later, her phone rang. It was Howie.

"Hi, babe. You finished with the paperwork?" He heard a slight silence on the phone. "Hello? Myami, are you there?"

"Yes! I'm here. I didn't have time to finish your homework."

"Why not?"

"I have a life too. I'm not here to do your homework. That's your job."

It was quiet once again on the phone. All of a sudden, the phone clicked. "Howie, Howie!" Myami yelled. "I know he didn't hang up on me," she said to herself. She threw the phone on the bed and continued lying down. She couldn't believe he had hung up on her because she didn't complete his assignment.

Later on that night, after not hearing from Howie, Myami turned off her phone and went to sleep.

———————

Myami hadn't spoken to Howie in two days. She thought about him more and more each day and wanted to reach out, but didn't. Both of them were being stubborn.

The next day, Myami went to work. Her eyes opened wide when she saw Howie in the break room warming up his food. Myami just knew today they would start speaking again.

She called her mom to vent about the way Howie was ignoring her. "Hi, Mom, you got a minute?" Myami asked, hoping her mother was free.

"Of course, baby. What's wrong?"

"Well, when I arrived to work, I walked into the break room and Howie was standing there warming up his food. When he was done, he walked right past me without saying a word to me." Myami was very hurt by his actions.

"It's his loss. You just have to move on. Don't cry over spilled milk."

Myami thought about what her mother stated. They talked for a few more seconds before hanging up. It was time for Myami to go back to work.

It had been a week and Myami still hadn't spoken with Howie. She decided to be the bigger person by picking up the phone and calling him. The phone rang at least four times. She was about to hang up, when a voice answered and said, "May I help you?"

"Howie, is this you?"

"Yes. What can I do for you?"

Myami hung up the phone and started crying. Her phone started ringing. She looked at the caller ID; it was Howie calling her back. "What's your problem?" he screamed at her.

"I don't have a problem, you do. Since I didn't complete your homework, you threw me to the wolves."

He started laughing and coughing. Myami didn't find anything funny. This was her first time crying over a boy. She had feelings for Howie and that made a difference.

"Let's go to the movies and talk about starting over again."

"Okay. Saturday, right?"

"Yep."

"I'll see you then." Myami was very excited about her upcoming date with Howie. Hopefully they could get past this incident.

———————————

Saturday had finally arrived and it was movie night. Howie was outside blowing the car horn. Myami's father was bothered by that. He believed a real man was supposed to knock on the front door and then walk to the car together after he had spoken to the parents. Myami heard her father telling her mother that. She texted Howie and told him to come inside. Howie knocked on the door and said hello to everyone. Myami looked at her dad and smiled. She gave her parents a kiss on the cheek and walked out of the house.

Howie laughed. "What was the text about?"

Myami smiled. "I overheard my father talking to my mom about you blowing the horn and not coming inside."

"Well, our plans have changed. We are going somewhere special."

Myami looked and asked, "Where?"

They pulled up in front of the Marriot Hotel.

Myami cleared her throat. "What is this?"

"Our special night that we will spend together."

Myami looked around the parking lot and gave him one of her fake smiles.

"I can't do this. I'm not that type of girl."

"What type of girl is that? We are here to be alone with one another, no strings attached."

They got out of the car and walked into the hotel. Myami was so nervous, she was shaking inside and out. After being checked into their room, they walked into the elevator and the doors closed, and it felt like her heart dropped. She walked around the room. Howie jumped on the bed and pulled off his sneakers. Myami sat in the chair with her legs closed and her pocketbook on her lap.

"Get comfortable. Stop acting all shy."

"Why are we here? I mean, really?"

He smirked and shook his head. As he started flipping through the channels, he grabbed a beer out of the refrigerator.

"What are you doing? You drink?" Myami asked, surprised by what she was seeing.

"On occasion." He smiled. "Get loose. You holding on to your purse like someone is going to snatch it."

Myami was sitting there, but she was ready to go. Howie started on his second beer. Myami was starting to get disgusted with his behavior.

"Myami, Myami come lay across the bed and let's watch some TV." Howie yelled out her name.

She walked over to the bed and sat on the edge of it. Howie pulled Myami by the arm. "Get over here," Howie playfully demanded.

Howie turned off the lights. He lay next to Myami and started kissing on her neck and rubbing her breast.

"Get off me. I don't want this," Myami yelled.

Howie moved over and continued drinking his beer.

"Have you ever tasted beer before?" he asked her.

"No."

He handed her the can and said, "Taste it."

It was nasty, but she continued drinking it. About an hour later, Myami asked Howie for a kiss. They started kissing. Howie started unfastening her blouse and moving his tongue down the middle of her chest. As he placed her right nipple in his mouth, she started making noise. He was rubbing his fingers through her hair and slowly pulled out the rubber band that held her ponytail together. Howie took off her blouse and she took off her pants. Howie couldn't believe this was happening. He undressed as he slowly pulled the cover over the both of them.

The foreplay was feeling good to Myami. She kept making noises and pulling his head towards her, while his face was between her legs. This was Myami's first sexual experience. Her legs were trembling and her eyes were going up into her head. She kept saying, "Please don't stop." Then Myami said the magic words, "I Love You." Howie lifted his head up, smiled, and kept going. He started kissing her on the mouth. Myami stopped and thought about allowing him to kiss her on the mouth after he had just gone down on her. Myami couldn't believe what had just happened.

"I never felt like that before," Myami gushed.

"It felt good, huh?" They both started laughing while lying there. They were officially boyfriend and girlfriend again. Myami jumped up and screamed about her curfew.

"Let's stay here overnight."

"I can't, I have a curfew. You must do this all the time."

"What you mean, *I do this all the time?*" He started shaking his head and laughing. "Well, can we take our first shower together?" Howie asked. They grabbed one another's hands and walked into the bathroom together.

––––––––––––

It had been almost two months and the relationship between Myami and Howie was stronger than ever. They did the majority of everything together.

One day Myami's mother was frying chicken. Myami walked down the stairs and asked her mom, "What is that stinking smell?"

"I don't know what you smell, but I smell chicken."

Myami started gagging and ran into the bathroom. Her mother knocked on the door. "Are you alright?"

"Yes," Myami yelled. Once done, she came out of the bathroom. "Mom, I think that chicken is spoiled. You really don't smell it?"

"No, I don't.

Weeks later, Myami still kept gagging every time she smelled a certain type of food. She decided to go to the doctor and get a checkup. They took a pregnancy test and it came back positive. She didn't know what to do. She could only burst out crying. All she could think about were her parents. Now she had to go home and tell her parents they were going to be grandparents. Before pulling off from the doctor's office, she sat in her car for fifteen minutes crying. She was nervous and didn't know what to do. Howie popped up in her mind. She asked herself, "What would Howie say?" She had so much going through her mind, she didn't know what to do.

Before getting out of the car, she drove around the block at least four times. She finally pulled up and got out of the car. "Mom! Dad! Where are you?" Myami called out.

They were in the family room watching TV. Myami sat in the chair and said out loud, "I can't believe it."

Her mom looked at her and asked, "What's wrong?"

Myami started crying with her head down.

"Did that boy Howie do something to you?" her dad asked.

"No! I'm having a baby."

Her father got up and walked out. Her mom asked, "You didn't use protection?"

"No, I didn't."

"Who's the father?"

"Mom! Howie is the only boy I've ever been with."

"How did he take the news?"

"I haven't told him yet. I just got the news today."

"Girl, you have to tell him and tell him soon," her mother replied.

"I was thinking about inviting him over for dinner to tell him."

Her mother looked at her and said, "You cook this time."

Myami smirked and shook her head.

"Well, I have to go talk to your father." Her mom walked out shaking her head.

Myami called Howie to check and see what he was doing. She also invited him to dinner the following week.

After talking to Howie, Myami decided to take a nap. She started feeling sick and was vomiting the next day. She called her mom to come upstairs. Her mom thought something was wrong by the way she was screaming.

"What's wrong with you, Jenni?"

"I don't feel good. I just vomited in the bathroom."

Her mother looked at her. "You are having a baby and that's a part of being pregnant." Her mom headed toward the door laughing. "This is just the beginning."

A week later, Howie came over to the house for dinner. Myami told him she needed to talk to him. Her mother and dad got up and walked out of the room.

Howie said, "What's going on, Myami? Your father just kept looking at me like I did something to him." Then he whispered to Myami, "You didn't tell them we had sex, did you?"

"Why would I tell my parents something like that? That is so not me." She smirked at him. "Well, I went to the doctor's last week because I wasn't feeling good. I took a pregnancy test and it came back positive."

Howie's eyes opened as wide as they could. "You are having my baby?" Howie asked.

"Yes," Myami replied.

They started hugging and crying at the same time.

"WOW!" Howie stated. "I'm going to be a father." He grabbed Myami's hand. "Let's go tell my mom."

"How will your mother feel? We only met twice. I don't want her to think I'm one of these fast ass girls."

Howie started smiling. "Come on."

As they were walking out the door, Myami said, "Mom I will be right back."

After arriving to Howie's mother's house, they sat down and told Howie's mom and she was so excited. She said, "You know, Howie, you have to step up and be a father. It's time to be

a man. You will have a big responsibility now, that's a baby."
They hugged one another. "I can't wait to spoil my grandchild."

Myami was now six months pregnant and she wanted to
have a baby shower. She invited Howie's mom over so that they
could plan a big baby shower. They planned the shower for
when she became seven months. As Myami's stomach started
getting big, everyone started getting excited.

The Baby Shower Day arrived. As the guests started
arriving, she started getting nervous, wondering what people
would say about her pregnancy. Myami received so many gifts,
she didn't have to buy anything for a couple of months after the
baby arrived.

The baby was born and they were so happy together as a
family. Howie thought it was time to get their own place.
Myami was a little hesitant, but she realized it was time for her
to grow up and take care of her family. They found an apartment
on the other side of town. Howie was still working, while
Myami stayed home taking care of their son.

One year later, Howie started drinking and smoking
weed with his friends. He would go to work late and he almost

got fired twice. The money slowed down and they had a hard time paying the bills. Myami decided to go to the welfare office to apply for some assistance. Howie didn't appreciate his baby's mother having to be on welfare.

Howie started getting out of control. He didn't allow any of Myami's friends in the house and he barely let her talk on the phone to them. He was always getting upset when she wanted to take the baby to go see her parents. They had started arguing frequently and it was turning into verbal abuse.

Myami needed to vent, so she called her mom and talked to her when he was at work. She felt like some days she was in jail and couldn't have any visitors. She really started stressing and losing weight.

She found out she was pregnant with her second child and only told her mom at first, and her mom begged her to get an abortion. A couple of weeks later, she told Howie. When she told him the news which she thought would help to calm him down some, the only thing that came out of his mouth was, "How can you have another child and I didn't marry you when you had the first one, whore?"

After she told her mother what Howie said, her mom really tried to talk her out of having this child. She felt that Myami didn't need another child at this time in her life.

Myami wanted to go back to college, but Howie wouldn't let her. He would always say to her, "A good mother stays home and takes care of her kids."

During this time, Myami started having issues with low self-esteem. She even thought about staying home and going to college online, but he wasn't having that either.

The arguments started progressing, especially in front of their kid. Howie would always put her down and call her every name in the book. She started enjoying the times when Howie wasn't at home. It felt so peaceful, just her and her child all alone.

One night, Myami cooked a big meal and Howie never came home. She kept calling and texting him, but he never answered. He walked through the door at three in the morning, smelling like a liquor store.

"Where were you?" Myami questioned.

"None of your business. I'm grown." He flopped on the bed and fell asleep. Later on that morning, he had to call off from work. Whenever Myami would walk past him, she shook her head. She fed her child and got him dressed to go to the doctor. Taking him to the doctors was one of the only ways she was able to stop by her mom's house. She stopped by her mother's house and her mom was so excited to see her and the baby.

When she returned home, Howie was still in bed smelling and looking like shit. She started thinking about her situation and what happened to their relationship. She thought about what her mom said, "He is too comfortable with you. A man will learn his woman's weakness and use it against her." Everything started running through her mind as she sat in the living room watching TV. She knew she had to get out of the relationship before he dragged her down with him.

One day, she had to sneak to her mom's house; she wanted to talk to her. It had gotten to the point that she couldn't call over the phone anymore because Howie would listen to their phone conversation. Pulling up in front of her parents' home, her mom was happy to see her and the baby. She could tell Myami wasn't happy at all. As a mother, she felt it. It was time for a long-overdue mother/daughter talk. She said, "Jenni, you never knew this, but I was wearing your shoes once upon a time.

Myami looked a little confused. "Mom, what are you talking about?"

Her mother cleared her throat and said, "Listen closely."

"When I was eighteen I fell in love with this guy named Roger. At first, we were so in love and happy with one another. He started hanging with a new group of people. Day by day, I saw the change in him. He started drinking and talking shit; it was like an everyday thing with him. I wasn't allowed to have friends, but he had them. He would constantly call me bitch, whore, fat-ass and tell me to Shut the Fuck up like I was trash. I didn't want him to be mad at me, so I would listen to him. In the beginning, it was just verbal abuse, then one day when I didn't come to his apartment, he thought I was with another guy and slapped me. From that day on, I feared him. He didn't want me to work at all. He had a part time job and we would go out to the movies on his pay day. I couldn't even speak to another boy. If I did, I wouldn't hear the end of it. I was the biggest whore in the world according to him. He would say, 'You had to have had sex with these guys, they not smiling for nothing.' I couldn't believe what he was putting me through. He hit me three times and after each time he would promise me that he would never do it again. I went through hell with him. A guy like that is so controlling and jealous. My friends thought it was love and that

47

he was strung out over me. I was stupid to stay in that type of relationship for three years. I had to learn the hard way that it wasn't love because love doesn't hurt.

"I'm glad you reached out to me. I didn't have anyone to talk to. It was verbal and physical abuse and no woman should go through that. A man that treats a woman like that needs help. I'm telling you this because you don't have to stay in that relationship. He doesn't love you, he wants to control you."

"Mom, I never knew this." Myami was shocked by her mother's admission.

"I knew you were going through this because I've been there and I know the signs. Get out before he hurts you and the baby. Remember, you can come back home anytime."

Three weeks later, Myami got a call from a girl who told her that she was in a relationship with Howie. Myami approached Howie about it, but he denied it. Myami called the girl while he was there. He still denied it while the girl was on the phone.

"She is trying to mess up our happy home!" Howie yelled. He grabbed the phone out of Myami's hand and hung it up. "Watch out for bitches like that. They only want to come between us."

She didn't believe him because when she asked the girl how she got the number, she said he always called her from this number. He slipped up this time and forgot to add the block feature when he called her. Myami left it alone. Instead, she packed her bags and the next day, while he was at work, she went to her mother's house.

When he arrived home and found her gone, he called her, yelling on the phone and calling her all types of stupid bitches. She stayed at her mom's house for one week and went back home. He made so many promises and she believed him.

Myami would often say, all she had was her kids and her dreams. She wanted to be a clothing designer and move to Florida. Her mother bought her a computer for Christmas so she could take designing classes online. Myami had to keep that a secret from Howie. She would do her classes while he was working. Each day before getting out of bed, she prayed that God would give her the strength to get out of this so-called relationship and follow her dreams.

Myami was no longer herself; it seemed like she had the world on her shoulders. She was trying to fight off the demons and her number one demon was Howie. She was getting bigger and feeling more tired. She didn't feel like cooking anymore or doing the cleaning around the house. She had her ups and downs and Howie didn't make it any better. The days Myami didn't cook, Howie would come home with food for him and his son. He thought it would bother Myami, but it didn't. She was tired of vomiting anyway. When he brought food home, Myami would call him stupid in her head because that's what she wanted him to do anyway.

She was ready to have the baby and start back doing her online classes. She was determined to make it in the world. She had income coming in from welfare that wasn't enough for her and her child. So, she knew it was not going to be enough when the second child was born. She decided to make another list of goals:

> *1-To Leave Howie*
> *2-To get off this system called welfare*
> *3-Move to Florida*
> *4-Live, Love, Life Again.*

Her mom thought it was time for her to get a cell phone, so she purchased her a phone. It was for emergencies only. Myami was happy. She never thought about getting one because she knew Howie wouldn't approve of it. Just as she was admiring her new phone, Howie walked through the door and saw the phone on the table.

"Myami, who was over here and left their phone?"

"No one. My mother bought me this phone for emergencies only."

"Did you tell your mom you needed a phone?"

"No, I was surprised when she gave it to me."

Howie walked in the room with an attitude. Howie never liked Myami being around her mom. He would always say that her mother was putting stuff in her head.

She had her second baby and everything was going great for about six months after the baby was born. Howie started back drinking and staying out all night again. She got tired of the arguing and the name calling. He had no respect for her anymore. All she could do was pray for better.

One night, Howie stayed out all night again and he came home in the morning smelling like God knows what. He started fussing and throwing things around in the room.

"Howie! What's wrong with you?"

"YOU! You are so bitchy!"

Myami didn't have any idea what his drunken ass was talking about.

"Please be quiet. The kids are sleeping."

"Fuck you and the kids!" Howie yelled out.

Myami jumped up. "What did you just say?" She walked closer to him. "You can disrespect me all you want, but don't you dare disrespect our kids. They are innocent!"

Howie looked at her. "How do I know these are my kids?"

Myami blew out some air to ease her nerves and walked into the kitchen. She stood in front of the stove crying. She couldn't believe what was coming out of his mouth. She wanted to call her mother and talk to her, but she couldn't. Howie walked into the kitchen, opened the refrigerator, and told Myami to make him some breakfast. As she walked out of the kitchen, she mumbled, "Tell the whore you were with to make you some breakfast."

He ran out of the kitchen and into the room. "What the hell did you say?"

"You heard me. If you want some breakfast, tell your whore to make it."

"That's why I'm asking you, Whore!"

Myami started thinking that it was time for her to get out of this fucked up relationship before she went to jail. Howie was just lying on the bed, laughing.

"Laugh now, cry later." Then she started laughing. She grabbed her weekend bag out of the closet.

He jumped up. "You ain't going nowhere."

"Get out of my face before I call the police."

"The police? For what we are talking about? Really Myami?"

Myami walked out of the room to check on her kids. They were still sleeping. She went back into her room and started packing her clothes.

"Howie, I can't take this anymore. You are a disrespectful asshole."

He grabbed her bag and started taking the clothes out and throwing them on the bed.

"Give me back my bag. I'm leaving."

"You are not going anywhere. Go sit your ass down somewhere!" he yelled.

She knew he wasn't going to let her leave, so she had to put her thinking cap on. She was determined to leave him. There was no doubt in her mind about that. She could see the scariness in Howie's eyes.

"I'm leaving you. If not today, then one day."

Howie turned around and slapped her so hard, she thought her nose was broken because of the blood. She ran in the bathroom to get a washcloth. As she looked in the mirror and saw the blood coming out of her nose, she screamed. "Ughhh!"

Howie started banging on the door. "Open the door! See what you made me do? I love you Myami. You are not taking the kids and going anywhere."

Myami took a deep breath and opened the door. She knew she was leaving, but she didn't know when.

Howie walked over to her. "I'm sorry. You know I didn't mean it." He tried to give her a kiss, but she turned her head.

Myami started thinking about her mom and the story she told her.

"Do you want me to make us some breakfast?" Howie asked, determined to make things right.

"You can make you and the kids some. I'm not hungry."

"You sure? I'm going to make an enough for the family." Then he walked out of the room.

Myami went back to look in the mirror and wash her face. She started praying, 'God, please give me the strength to take my kids and leave Howie.' She prayed every morning and night about it. She heard the phone ringing.

Howie yelled, "Babe, answer the phone. It's your mom."

"I'll call her back." She didn't want to speak to her mom because of what had just happened. She sat on the bed. She couldn't believe that Howie thought everything was okay. She just smiled and walked out the room. She checked on the kids and proceeded to the kitchen. Howie walked over to her and tried to kiss her, but she walked away.

"Are you going to have an attitude all day?"

"If I do, you will smack me again."

"No. I would never hit you again."

She wanted to believe that, but at that time she didn't trust anything he said. She started hating him and wishing bad things on him. She took all that back because of Karma.

One month later, Myami had taken the kids to her mom's house for the weekend. Howie and Myami wanted to spend time alone. Howie was excited. Myami couldn't stand the ground he walked on. Yes, it had gotten that bad.

Myami's phone rang and Howie answered it. It was a guy on the other end who had the wrong phone number. Howie was pissed off. He accused Myami of cheating on him. She thought it was funny, so she started laughing.

"Oh, you think this is funny?"

"Howie, hush. That's your conscience messing with you." She looked at his face and she saw the veins busting out on his forehead. Myami realized he wasn't playing. Every time he got mad those same veins appeared across his forehead.

"Myami, you think this is a joke?"

"No. I'm not paying you no attention."

He walked over to her and grabbed her hair.

"What are you doing? Are you crazy?" She screamed. "Get the hell off my hair!"

"First tell me, who was the dude on the phone?"

She was crying and screaming at the same time. "I don't know! I don't know!"

Howie let go of her hair and slapped her in the face. She ran into the bedroom, then closed and locked the door. He started banging on the door.

"Open this damn door, bitch!"

"Howie, I don't know that guy who called here!"

"You lying bitch!"

She turned on the TV and started watching it. She knew she had to wait for him to calm down. She fell asleep for a while until she heard a loud bang on the door. It was Howie.

"I'm sorry, baby. I love you so much!"

"Howie, I'm tired of being abused, I can't do this no more. I have to think of my safety and my kids' safety first."

He started banging on the door again. "Open this damn door before I break it down."

"I'm calling the police." She picked up the phone and pretended to call so he could hear the dial tone. After that it was quiet, so she figured he left the apartment. She opened the bedroom door and looked around. There was no sight of Howie. She looked out the living room window and saw him pulling off. "I hate you!" she yelled out.

She called her mother and told her mom what happened.

"Jenni, get out of that apartment and don't look back."

"Mom, I'm so happy the kids weren't here. I'm going to be okay. I will come pick up the kids tomorrow afternoon."

"I think it's best if the kids stay here."

"No, I'm coming to get them tomorrow. He would never hurt his kids." She hung up and thought about it. "Nah he won't hurt his kids," she said as she shook her head. She turned on her computer and went to her notes and wrote things down. She had it all planned out. She knew that they couldn't be together any longer. Her plan was to pick up her kids so he could spend one last night with them. She had purchased train tickets to Florida to stay with her aunt until she got on her feet. Her aunt owned a daycare, so childcare wouldn't be a problem for her. Myami and her aunt kept this secret. She didn't even tell her mom. Myami made herself something to eat and then went to bed.

Howie finally came in the house around one am smelling his usual way. Myami was pretending to be asleep so there wouldn't be any drama.

The next morning, Myami got up and told Howie she was going to pick the kids up at her mom's. He told her to bring some breakfast back and gave her twenty dollars. She arrived at her mother's house as if nothing had happened the day before. She wanted to tell her mom so bad she was getting out of the relationship and going to live with her aunt in Florida. She planned this so carefully. Her plan was to call her mother once she reached Florida.

After packing the kids up, Myami looked at her mom. "Don't worry, we are going to be okay." She gave her mom a kiss on the cheek. "I love you and stop worrying."

Myami stopped at McDonalds for some breakfast. She couldn't wait for Howie to go to work the following morning. She tried to avoid getting into any arguments with Howie that whole day. He played with the kids while she cooked dinner later that evening. Myami asked herself, "Why couldn't he be like this all the time?"

The next morning, Howie was up getting ready for work. "Myami, are you woke?"

Myami turned around to look at him. "Yes."

"I'm sorry for everything I've done lately. I just want us to be a happy family." He gave her a kiss on the mouth. "I will see you and the kids later."

He walked out of the room and she said softly under her breath, "No you won't." She waited for about thirty minutes and then took a shower. After that, she started packing everything she and the kids would need. She had her car shipped to Florida and they took Uber to the train station. She was so happy that morning. She felt like some of the weight had been lifted.

Myami finally made it to her aunt's house. She called her parents and told them everything. They were so happy for her, but they wished she would have told them what was going on. She changed her number on the way to Florida and told her mom not to give it to anyone.

Later that day, her car came. She saw this as a change for the better. She realized things happened for a reason. She had to go through her trials and tribulations to get out of a bad situation. While talking to her aunt, Myami stated, "No woman should have to go through any type of abuse."

Breaking Barriers: Family Secrets

By

Alma Collins Thomas

Alma Collins Thomas is an ordained Minister, Educator, Motivational Speaker, Playwright and Author. She holds two B.S Degrees, one in Human Services with a concentration in Children and Families and a BS in Christian Studies. She is a contributor writer for Authentically You and Strawberry-Lit Magazines. She is the co-author of several books including Love, Marriage and Divorce. I am and Sisters with Purpose. She is currently working on her two debut books "Dream Killers" and "From the Waiting Room to the Recovery Room." She is the single mother of two children Sabria and Tysean who left his earthly home to reign in his heavenly home in 2009

Charlisa Winfield stepped onto the elevator of the tenth floor. She was so excited that this hell of a day was finally over and she was heading home. When she entered the elevator it was full, but she still managed to squeeze into the elevator. She was so tired that she didn't even want to wait for another elevator. She felt so self-conscious that she looked at the floor the entire ride down. As soon as the elevator stopped on the ground floor, she hurried out. She had a long commute home to Long Island. She got into her 2017 Mercedes Benz E class and drove out of the parking garage. She finally began to relax when she turned onto the Grand Central Parkway. "Cirrus find WBGO 88-3." She was listening to Billie Holiday's 'For all we know' and she continued her long drive home.

She almost screamed halleluiah when she came to exit 30 on the Southern State Parkway. She was finally at home. She pulled into her circular driveway surrounding her eight-bedroom mansion, turned off the ignition, and sat in her car for a while. She was too tired to walk to her door. After a few minutes, she got out of the car and walked slowly up the stairs huffing and puffing all the way up. She quickly put her key in the door and pushed in the alarm code, then she cut off the alarm system and entered her spacious living room. She pulled off her blazer, tossed it over the leather recliner in the living room, went straight to the wine rack, and poured herself a Red Zinfandel. She promised herself after she rededicated herself to the Lord that she was going to stop drinking, but nowadays she wasn't drinking anything stronger than wine and she limited herself to no more than two glasses a night. She needed it to unwind especially after the long day that she had today.

She lit a candle and lay down on her Italian leather sofa. She looked around the room and noticed that she had a lot of material things, but nobody to share it with. She quickly drank the last of the wine and as soon as she finished, she had to go to the bathroom. She jumped off the couch and ran into the bathroom. As she passed the full-length mirror and saw her reflection, she hated what she saw. She was fifty-nine and she weighed 285 pounds.

As she was sitting on the toilet she thought about this journey called life. Despite all the education and material things she possessed, she still struggled with self-esteem and weight issues.

After she was done in the bathroom she went back into the living room and just sat down on the couch, laid her head back, closed her eyes, and her mind started to wander. She thought about last year and how traumatic it had been for her. She recently rededicated her life back to the Lord and rejoined her father's church, Little Shepherd Christian Outreach Ministries in Amityville New York where her father was the presiding Bishop. She rejoined the church after she had finally had enough and broke it off with Anthony. She discovered that he was a con artist and had wives in California, Georgia and Alabama. When she read the police write up on Anthony she found out that Anthony Johnson was just one of the aliases that he used. He preyed on women with low self-esteem issues. Charlisa had invested thousands of dollars buying him clothes for imaginary job interviews, paying his cell phone bills so she would always have a way to get in touch with him and even then, she had a hard time tracking him down.

When he gave her an engagement ring, he stood a chance of being able to claim half of what she was worth if she had married him. She was lucky that she dodged that bullet, but she did not feel lucky when she found out the truth about him. Her father hired one of the private investigators that they used for the law firm to follow Anthony, and the pictures of Anthony that the investigator showed her turned her stomach even now, a year later.

She thought that Anthony was honoring her wishes to stay celibate until marriage, but the real deal was he was not sexually attracted to her. He was attracted to her name and her net worth, but he was sleeping with different women all over the United States. She was totally disgusted and humiliated when the private investigator showed her the pictures and she was relieved when he was arrested for tax evasion and numerous other charges. Her father was right— a man as fine as Anthony only wanted her for her money.

All of these horrible memories were adding to her migraine headache, a headache that she had gotten earlier in the day from her father and his constant criticism of her and everything that she did. Nothing was good enough for old

Caliphs Winfield. She had worked her behind off to become a partner in her father's law firm.

You would have thought that her last name would make it easier for her, but instead it made it harder for her. The road for her was full of twists, turns, and sand obstacles, but eventually all of her blood, sweat, and tears lead to her being a partner at Winfield, Dotson, Thomas and Winfield, the prestigious law firm in the heart of Manhattan. The law firm had handled many of the current cases against the NYPD police killings against unarmed black men in Black Men Matter cases. Charlisa was the leading defense lawyer in many of these cases and she had won large sums of money against the city of New York, but that still wasn't good enough for her father. Ever since Charlisa was a little girl it was her dream to work alongside her father in his law firm. Her father did not try any cases anymore since becoming the prelate of their churches, but he still ran the office. Nothing transpired that he did not approve of. Charlisa was often the cause of her father's disproval.

Charlisa graduated valedictorian from high school, Magna Cum Laude from college, she graduated Cum Laude from Harvard Law School, and still none of this impressed her father. Despite all of her achievements she could never be what her father wanted—her brother as a partner so he could eventually become head partner and take over the law firm one day. But that would never happen. Her brother Charles had dropped out of Law School in his second year after a scandal involving him and a male professor at the Law School who was promptly fired. Currently, her brother was a writer for Trendy Magazine that catered to the Gay and Lesbian community. Her brother had even thought about a sex change operation, but later changed his mind.

Today in the office, all hell broke loose. Today was the first time in almost a year that her father and brother had seen each other. Charles had invited her to lunch today and she told him that she would meet him in the restaurant, but he insisted on coming to the office. It was Thursday and the only day that her father even visited the law firm was sometimes on Tuesday to sign off on papers, but today of all days he had a meeting. He decided to meet in the conference room of the law firm. As Charles entered the office he ran right straight into Caliphs.

Charles said, "Hello, Dad. How are you? Long time no see."

Charlisa could see the look of pure hate in his eyes and he growled, "Don't ever call me Dad! You are not my son. I don't know who are, but I do know that you are an abomination to God and an embarrassment to me and the entire family. You are as good as dead to me."

"I am sorry that I have never been good enough for you, and we all have skeletons in our closet, don't we Dad? But I will never be able to fill your shoes, neither have I ever wanted to."

Caliphs replied, "I don't ever want to see you again. You are not welcome at this firm or at my home, do you hear me? You are as good as dead to me."

"I am sure you wish I was dead because I remind you of your sins."

Caliphs grew angrier and angrier. "Get the hell out of my office!"

Charles ran out of the office never looking back. Charlisa started to run after him, but she was out of breath by the time she ran down the first flight of stairs. She sat down on the landing huffing and puffing and calling after Charles, but Charles continued running down the three flights of stairs and out into the parking garage. Charlisa tried calling his phone several times during the day, but he never picked up the phone and it went directly to voicemail. Replaying the events of the day made her head hurt worse than ever and she was just about to take an aspirin, when the shrill ringing of the phone startled her. She answered the phone without checking the caller ID thinking it might be Charles, but as soon as she heard her mother's voice on the other end of the phone she was immediately sorry that she had not checked the caller ID.

"Hello, Mother."

"Hi Charlisa," her mother relied. Then she lit into Charlisa. "Your father told me what happened at the office today. Why did you have to meet your brother at the office? You know that he and your father are not seeing eye to eye right now, so it's best that they avoid each other."

"Wait a minute, Mother." She was trying to be respectful, but like always, her mother was getting on her nerves. "First of all, Mother, Dad never comes into the office any day other than Tuesdays. Secondly, Charles is the one that insisted on meeting me at the office."

"You set your brother up and you should be ashamed of yourself. You were always jealous of your brother."

"Goodnight, Mother." She did not wait for her to answer before she quickly hung up the phone. Charlisa and her mother never really got along and her mother always found a way to blame anything that happened on Charlisa and made it her fault. She always favored and babied Charles and she was always really hard on Charlisa.

After Charlisa hung up on her mother she was feeling really hungry. She was going to drink a protein shake and eat a salad, but now her stomach was growling, so she decided to order Chinese food and have it delivered. She ordered a sampler platter for two. Two eggs rolls, an order of chicken wings, shrimp fried rice, and a diet coke. She went back into the living room and sat down on the couch to wait for her food to be delivered.

After forty-five minutes, she heard the doorbell ring. She went to the door and said, "Who is it?" When she heard "delivery," she opened the door, handed the man the money, and grabbed the food. She took the bag into the large, contemporary kitchen, sat at the huge table that was set for eight, and piled all of the food onto a pretty China plate before she shoveled the food into her mouth like she had not had a hot meal in years. Before she realized it, she had polished off the entire order—enough food for four people.

She got up from the table and went straight into the bathroom, closed the door, and bent over the toilet. She put her finger down her throat and brought up all the food that she had just eaten. She washed out her mouth and went into her bedroom with tears in her eyes, promising herself that this would be the last time that she would ever do this. Every time she did it, she regretted it and promised herself that she was not going to do it again.

Charlisa took off her clothes, walked into her luxurious master bathroom, and climbed into the shower. She turned the water on as hot as she could take it and she let the water cascade over her ample body, relaxing more and more with each drop. She stayed in the shower for at least an hour. When she stepped out of the shower she had almost forgotten all of the painful events of the day, but that peace was going to be short-lived because as soon as she made it to her bedroom the phone was ringing.

She looked at the ID this time and it was her mother again. She decided to just answer the phone or her mother would call all night. "Hello Mother."

"Why did you hang up that phone in my face?"

"I did not hang up on you. I said goodnight, which is the logical end to a conversation."

"Don't try to use that legal mumbo jumbo with me, young lady. I will slap the black off you. I just called to see what you had for dinner tonight. You know the doctor said that you had to lose weight and your father said when he saw you today at the office you looked like a butterball stuffed in that suit. And as long as you weigh a ton you will never find a man that is going to take a second look at you. No intelligent man wants to be seen with you. All of those eligible bachelors in the church and none of them would take a second look at you. Yesterday Calvin and Ashley got engaged. Do you know how that makes us look? All of those young women are getting married right around you and you haven't had a date since that con artist. So, what did you eat tonight?"

Charlisa answered her in a barely audible voice, "I had a protein shake and a salad."

"What did you eat? I cannot hear you."

She repeated it again, this time louder. "I had a salad and a protein shake."

"I hope you keep it up. All of your life you have been starting fad diets and never finishing them."

"Goodnight, Mother. I am going to bed because I have to be in court early in the morning."

"By the way, have you talked to your brother tonight?"

"No, I tried all night and his phone is still going to voicemail." Charlisa hung up the phone and sat staring at the phone for what seemed like forever. She closed her eyes and tried to fall asleep, but she couldn't, so she decided to go into the kitchen to get a bottle of water. She opened the refrigerator and looked at the water, but closed the door. Instead she opened the cabinet and reached behind all of the Weight Watchers and Slim Fast products to her stash of golden Oreo cookies. She opened the package and took out two cookies, quickly stuffed them into her mouth, and decided to take the whole bag into her bedroom. As she passed the freezer she took out the half gallon of golden vanilla ice cream.

She took all of her goodies into her bedroom. As she sat down she said, "Darn, I forgot to get a spoon." She opened her nightstand drawer and took out a plastic spoon. She sat in the middle of her bed and quickly finished off all of the cookies and ice cream. Once done, she got out of the bed and went into the bathroom, closed the door, and for the second time that night, she stuck her finger down her throat and threw up everything that she just ate. She leaned against the door and started crying and praying. "God, please help me. I can't keep doing this." After each time she did it, her throat was starting to feel a little more irritated.

She quietly slipped back into bed with tears flowing down her cheeks. She could not, as much as she tried, cut off her thoughts. She was so lonely. Was her mother right? Was her weight keeping her from having a meaningful relationship?

For the last month, she had been using a dating site. She had talked with several guys on the phone, but she had not met anybody in person yet. She was so skeptical after

Anthony. She opened her cell phone and tapped on her email account. She saw that she had a new message from Donald 546. He was very handsome in his profile picture. His description said that he was 6ft 3inches and that he was loving and caring with a good sense of humor. He was a Christian that attended church twice a week.

His message said, "Hello, how are you? I like your profile. Do you have a picture?"

Charlisa closed the email and said, "Well here we go." She had fudged her profile just a little. She cut off the light and finally drifted off to sleep.

She awoke to the sound of her alarm going off. She blinked her eyes several times, trying to focus on the time, and she finally saw that it was five fifteen. She decided that she would get up so she could stop by her brother's apartment in Garden City before she went to court this morning. She was doing the closing arguments in the police brutality case.

She slowly swung her feet out of the bed and was searching for her slippers with her feet. She found her slippers and stepped into them. She then went into the bathroom and got into the shower. As she was stepping into the shower, she looked at her reflection in the mirror and once again she hated what she saw. She thought, "Why did I let myself go? Why do I always use food as a defense mechanism?"

After a quick shower, Charlisa stepped out of the shower and dried herself off. She tried to cover her body with the extra-large towel, but she could not get it to close. She went back into her bedroom to get dressed.

After the conversation with her mother last night, she felt so self-conscious in every outfit that she tried on. She finally decided on a black pantsuit with a purple blouse that hid her stomach. She looked at herself in the mirror. "I look good today. This suit makes me look ten pounds lighter. She went back into her bedroom to get her pocketbook and cell phone. When she picked up her cell phone, she decided to try to call her brother again.

She dialed his phone and again it went straight to voicemail. Now she was getting worried. No matter what her brother was going through with the family he always answered her call. Despite the lies that her mother told, she and Charles had a close relationship. She had long gotten over the fact that he was their mother's favorite. She knew that yesterday, after what had transpired between him and their father, that he was really upset so she wanted to give him a little time to cool off. She dialed his friend Diego's number.

He answered, "What up, Charlisa?"

"Have you heard from Charles?"

"He called me earlier yesterday and said he had a big blowout with your father and that this was the last time that he was going to allow your father to treat him like dirt. And something about him not being the man that everybody thought he was and one day he was going to get what was coming to him. He hung up and I haven't been able to reach him since."

Charlisa hung up from Diego and she did not have a good feeling about this at all. She had to be in court at 9:15, but she was definitely going to stop by her brother's first.

She got into her car and was heading down the Southern State Parkway. She looked at the speedometer and she was going almost ninety. She said aloud, "I better slow down before I get a ticket," but she felt like she had to get to her brother's in a hurry. She had such an eerie feeling, a feeling that she could not explain. She had never felt this way before. She was nervous when she drove into his circular driveway.

Charlisa got out of the car and hurried up the steps. She knocked on the door and then she banged on the door like the police. There was still no answer, so she took out her spare key and opened the door. She went in and as soon as she entered the living room, she let out the loudest shriek that she had ever heard. Lying on the living room floor was her brother Charles with several empty pill bottles scattered around him. Her lawyer skills kicked in. She had to get herself together.

She checked Charles' throat and felt a slight pulse. She pulled out her phone and dialed 911. "I need an ambulance to 703 Morningside Lane. My brother is unresponsive. He took some pills. Please hurry."

As she was waiting for the ambulance she was holding Charles' hand and calling his name. She started praying. "Father, in the name of Jesus, forgive me for all of my sins and please touch my brother. Please don't let him die."

The ambulance arrived and she decided to follow the ambulance to the hospital. As she was pulling out of the driveway behind the ambulance, she called her mother. "Mommy, meet me at Nassau Community Hospital in East Meadow. They are transporting Charles there and he is very sick." Her mother tried to ask her questions. "Mom just get to the hospital! It is bad really bad. Charles tried to kill himself."

Charlisa followed the ambulance to the emergency room parking lot and she jumped out of the car in time to see that they were still performing CPR on Charles. They rushed Charles into the emergency room and directed her to the emergency room waiting area. Charlisa sat down in the crowded waiting room and took out her phone to text one of the other partners in the firm to tell them where her depositions were and to ask them to go to court to get the case postponed because she had an emergency.

The room was crowed, but she didn't make eye contact with anybody. She sat, staring at her phone. She noticed as she was checking her emails that she had another email from David 546. "Good morning, beautiful. Still waiting on that picture." Just as she was turning off her phone, she heard her mother screaming.

"Where is my baby? Where is he?" Lady Theresa, under normal circumstances, was a drama queen. She ran over to the desk. "Charles Winfield, that's my baby. Take me to him! I want to see my baby right now!"

The nurse at the desk said, "I have paged the doctor and he will be out to talk to you in a minute. The young lady that came in with your son is sitting over there." She pointed to Charlisa.

Her mother glanced her way and quickly turned back to the nurse. "I want to see my son."

In a stern voice the nurse responded, "I told you that the doctor will be out to see you. Please have a seat in the waiting room."

Her mother rolled her eyes and found a seat across from Charlisa and without warning she blurted out, "Well Charlisa, I hope that you are happy now."

Charlisa was fed up with her mother. "Mother, please, you have to be freaking kidding me right now. Stop the theatrics and saying this is my fault. I told you yesterday that Charles insisted on coming to the office. If you are such a First Lady, why don't you shut up and pray?"

Lady Theresa had an astonished look on her face. Charlisa had never spoken to her like that before. Lady Theresa rolled her eyes. "I don't know who you are talking to, young lady. You must have lost your mind!"

Charlisa murmured under her breath, "Crazy recognizes crazy." Charlisa got up and went to the window. She looked out the window trying to keep from crying. This family was so dysfunctional that they couldn't come together even in a crisis. And noticeably missing was her father. Even if he did not approve of his son's lifestyle, he was still his son and he was lying back there clinging to life. Their father's pride would not allow him to come to the hospital. On so many occasions, perfect strangers would call her father and ask him for prayer and he would run to the hospital no questions asked, but his own son was lying at death's door and he was not here. When she looked up from her phone, she noticed that a group of doctors had gathered around her mother. She walked over and stood on the outside of the circle. She heard the doctors talking to her mom.

"Your son is very sick and the next twenty-four hours are critical. We have him in a medically induced coma. If he makes it through this critical period, we will slowly start to wake him up," Dr. Stein, the head doctor, stated. "You can go in one at a time to see him, but don't stay long because we want him to rest.

Charlisa just stared into space as her mother followed the doctor to the ICU unit. Charlisa stood there for a few minutes and then she went back to sit in the waiting room. After a few minutes she noticed that her mother had returned to the waiting room, but she did not say a word to Charlisa. Charlisa got up from her seat and walked down the corridor to ICU. The nurse was checking Charles' vitals. She looked up when she saw Charlisa.

"You can come in, but you can only stay for a few minutes. He needs his rest."

When Charlisa walked over to Charles' bed, she gasped. Charles was hooked up to so many machines, wires, and cords were coming out of every part of his body. The room was quiet except for the noise of the machines that were keeping Charles alive. Charlisa held Charles' hand and sat down in the chair next to the bed.

"Charles, can you hear me? If you hear me, please squeeze my hand." Charles did not move. "Please, Charles, do not stop fighting. You are a survivor, you are an overcomer, you have overcome so many obstacles in your life. Please don't give up now. I understand why you did it. Why you thought that this was your only way out. You are stronger than I am. So many times I considered ending it all. In reality, I am no different than you. I think that I am slowly killing myself with my binging and overeating. We have the residue from our past all over us and we just can't seem to shake our past. For years, we have both, in different ways, fought for our parents' love and affection. God is a forgiving God and he will forgive you for all of your sins. Please don't stop fighting. I do not know what I would do if I lost you." She kissed her brother on the forehead just as the nurse was coming back into the room to tell her that she had to leave. "I am on my way out. Thank you for everything."

Charlisa walked out of the room with tears flowing down her face. She could not stop crying because she hated to see her brother in that condition. She walked back into the waiting room. She scanned the room for her mother and saw her sitting in the corner talking loudly to someone on the phone. When she looked up and saw Charlisa, she started whispering.

Charlisa walked to the cafeteria. All of this commotion had her feeling hungry. She picked up a tray and ordered fried chicken, an order of fries, and a large milkshake. She sat where she could watch the door just in case her mother came into the cafeteria and caught her eating all the unhealthy foods. She quickly gobbled up all of the food on her plate, jumped up, and ran to the bathroom. She quickly checked the room to make sure that no one was in there, then she stuck her finger down her throat and threw up all of the contents of her stomach. As she left the bathroom, she looked at herself in the mirror and tears were coming down her face. "I cannot keep doing this. I need help." The smell of throw-up was pungent in her nostrils. At that moment, she hated herself and her life, but it was not about her. It was about Charles and him surviving this ordeal.

She looked in her pocketbook for her cell phone and called another one of the partners in the firm and asked him if he could take over her cases because her brother was in the hospital. After leaving the message she noticed that she had an email from Donald 546. "Hi, beautiful. I am still waiting." Charlisa was getting tired of this cat and mouse game, so she decided to send him a picture of her, and when he saw her picture he would be sickened at the sight of her. She looked through her photos and found a full-length photo of herself outside of the courtroom and pressed send.

Charlisa looked up from her phone. She thought she saw her father walking into the hospital. She waited for a few minutes in the cafeteria and then she went back into the waiting room. She looked into the corner and her mother wasn't in her seat, and she did not see any sign of her father in the waiting room. Before she went to her brother's room, she went by the vending machine and bought three snickers, two packs of chocolate chip cookies, and a pack of cheddar cheese potato chips. She stuffed all her goodies into her Michael Kors pocketbook and went to ICU to see if there had been any change in her brother's condition.

She walked swiftly down the hall to her brother's room, huffing and puffing. She was out of breath. All of this walking had her tired; she had not walked this much in her life. When she approached her brother's room, she could hear her parents' voices. It appeared like they were in a heated argument. She decided not to go right into the room, so she stood by the door listening to her parents' conversation. All her parents ever did was argue for the last twenty years. They never agreed on anything. If her mother said the sun was shining, her father would say that it was raining. The only time that they were not arguing was when they were in public. They put on an act for her father's law friends, the church, and outside family members. Everyone thought they were the Christian Huxtables.

She heard her mother say, "You hated Charles, not for what he was, but because he was a reminder of what you really are."

Now Charlisa was really listening. She moved closer to the door's entrance, but she made sure she was out of the sight of her parents.

"You are the one that did not live up to your end of the bargain, running all over town like a jezebel. You were supposed to be discreet. You were only supposed to give me one child to be the heir of my empire. How did you think I felt when I found out that the boy was not mine? And then I had to pay millions of dollars to protect your dirty secret."

"I was not the only one with a dirty little secret. How do you think it made me feel as a mother to cover up the things that you were doing to my son?"

"It made you look like the money-hungry harlot that you are. You practically blackmailed me every time I was ready to leave. You said you would tell the police and tell the world my secret, but I would put a few million dollars in your personal bank account and you were more than happy to keep up this façade."

"You are nothing more than a closet homosexual!"

"And you, my dear, are a heartless gold-digger."

Charlisa wanted to run into that room and slap those two strangers that, for thirty years, she had called mom and dad. Who in the heck were these people and what were they talking about? What she did understand was that Caliphs was not her or Charles' biological father. This all sounded like a Lifetime movie, but it wasn't a movie, it was her life.

As she was deciding whether or not to go into the room, she heard her father say softly, "I asked God to forgive me many years ago."

"But you never made it right with Charles. You made it seem like it was his fault, but he was the victim. You never broke the barrier of why we really got married. You continued the cycle and now look what it has caused." Out of nowhere, Lady Theresa grabbed Caliphs' neck and started choking him. He was gasping for air, trying to fight her off. Charlisa ran into the room.

"Stop it, Mother! What are you doing?"

At that time, the nursing staff ran into the room and Charles' machines were going off. Lady Theresa calmed down, and the doctor called code blue and ordered everybody out of the room. The doctors looked at her parents and said, "This is the hospital, not the wife wrestling arena. This young man is very sick. Please leave the room, all of you."

As Charlisa was leaving the room, she saw the doctors shock Charles' heart and she yelled, "Oh my goodness, my brother is dying."

The nurse came over and escorted her out of the room and security came and asked them all to go to the waiting room.

The security guard came to escort them out. "Your son being sick is the only reason why I am not making you leave the hospital, but if you do not behave yourself you are out of here."

"Rental cop, you must not know who I am. No one threatens me or my family. I will have your fake badge," Caliphs stated.

"Dad, please stop making a scene. Let's just go into the waiting room so we can wait for the doctors."

They all walked quietly to the waiting room and just as they were walking into the waiting room, their names were being paged over the loud speaker to go to the family counseling room on the third floor.

They ran toward the elevator. Her parents got there first and had to wait for her.

"Hurry up. You are so out of shape, it is surprising that you haven't had a heart attack yet," Lady Theresa said.

Charlisa ignored her mother and got on the elevator. Her father pushed the button for the third floor. They rode to the third floor in complete silence. They walked down the long sterile hallway until they found the door that said 'Family Consultation Room.' They knocked on the door.

"Come in and have a seat," Dr. Stern offered.

When they all sat down, Doctor Stern said, "Are you all the immediate family?"

Lady Theresa said, "Yes, I am his mother and this is his father, Caliph, and that his younger sister Charlisa."

Doctor Stern sat down and said, "There is no easy way to tell you this but straight. Charles is very sick. He is being kept alive with the breathing machine. He lost a great deal of oxygen and he's brain dead. He is being kept alive with the machine. Do you know if Charles signed a Durable Power of Attorney for Health Care?"

Lady Theresa was crying hysterically and Caliphs was just staring at the floor.

"What is his prognosis?"

Dr Stein said, "As I stated earlier, he is brain dead. Being brain dead is the complete and irreversible cessation stopping all brain function. We just did an EEG on him and he has been seen by the best neurologist in this hospital. We are flying in the best neurologist in the country. He should he here in forty-five minutes. He is officially diagnosed as brain dead. There is basically no chance of recovery. I am sorry."

"I have heard many stories of people coming out of comas and going on to live productive lives."

Dr Stern said, "Yes, but Charles is not in a coma, he is brain dead and there is a difference between a coma and being brain dead."

"So what are our options?" Charlisa went on.

"You can wait for the neurologist that is flying in. We have already determined that he is brain dead. After we receive the results from his tests, then you can decide if you want to pull the plug. I am going to leave you alone to talk and I am going to see if Dr Hong has gotten here yet."

When the doctor closed the door, Caliphs said, "I think we should pull the plug. Charles would not want to live like that."

Lady Theresa said, "You have always wanted him dead. You will pull the plug over my lifeless body."

Caliphs whispered, "If only it was that easy."

"What did you say?"

"Nothing at all."

Charlisa just sat there not really knowing what to say, so she took out her phone and started playing games on her phone. While she was playing on the phone she noticed that she had a message from David 546. "I guess this is his message saying that I am not the type of woman that he is looking for. He will say 'let's be friends' and then he will never message me again." She opened the message.

"Hello, beautiful. How are you doing? I can't lie. I got your picture and at first I was a little taken aback because that is not how I pictured you and I am usually not attracted to BBWs, but there is something about you that is telling me I need to get to know you better. My real name is David Hodges and my cell phone number is 347-555-5765. Call me anytime."

Charlisa thought to herself, "I am not calling him. He must be another con artist trying to get my money. Been there, done that." She closed the phone and wished she could eat the goodies in her pocketbook, but she dared not open her pocketbook in front of her mother.

"Mom, I will be right back. I have to use the bathroom."

Lady Theresa never looked up and she did not say anything so Charlisa left the room to look for the bathroom. When she went into the bathroom she looked around, went into a stall, and took out the snickers. She quickly ate the cookies and the chips and flushed the papers down the toilet because she did not want anyone to know that she was eating in the bathroom stall. How unsanitary was that? After she finished flushing the wrappers down the toilet, she kneeled over the toilet bowl and once again she forced herself to throw up. She went to the sink and washed out her mouth. She went back into the family consultation room and found her mother deep in thought.

Lady Theresa's thoughts took her back to years ago, when she was a little girl in Itta Bena, Mississippi. She was born Beulah Mae Jones. She was overweight as a teenager and her mother was a madam at a brothel. She started in the family business at an early age. She remembered the first trick that she turned like it happened yesterday and it still repulsed her.

All the other girls were already taken so her mother said, "Girl, you are going to earn your keep today. It takes a million dollars just to feed your fat butt."

When Beulah walked into the room, the john said, "This must be a joke. I asked for one of your prettiest woman, not your fattest cow."

Her mother apologized to the john and she heard her say, "She is a virgin and she will do anything and I mean anything that you want her to do."

She was thinking, "What kind of mother would make her own daughter do these nasty things with this decrepit old man?" She hated her mother and she hated her life. It was then that she began to work on a plan that she would leave this town and this house forever. She would not look back and certainly not return here. She started to make herself over. She lost over a hundred pounds and started turning tricks on her own and saving the money under the old mattress in her room.

The night she met Caliphs was when her big break came. She met him in a hotel room in Jackson, Mississippi and he paid her five hundred dollars. All he wanted to do was talk. She met him several times over the next few months. Whenever he was in town he would meet her. The meeting place upgraded from the seedy motel to a five-star hotel, but he still just wanted to talk. He told her that he was in law school and that his family had law firms in Washington DC and New York and that they handled all the civil rights cases. His family was one of the first black millionaires in America and he came from a long line of lawyers.

Then one day he told her his secret—that he did not like women, but he could never live out his passion because his family would disown him. They might even kill him because he was the only son and he had to inherit the family business.

Now, she was going by the name Theresa Crawford and she had graduated from the University of Mississippi School of Law. Several years ago, she stopped tricking and started working as a law clerk as she earned her law degree. She fabricated a story about her past. She said she was raised by her elderly grandmother who died five years ago, and she worked and paid her way through school. No one knew about her humble beginnings and her secret life but Caliphs. And no one knew about Caliphs' secret appetite but her.

When Caliphs graduated from Law School he introduced her to his parents as the refined lady that she was. After they were married, Caliphs never enjoyed having sex with her, but he wanted an heir to his throne. They were married for two years and she still had not gotten pregnant. She was a woman that had a high sex drive and needed more than Caliphs was willing to do. They only had sex when she was ovulating. He made her go to a fertility clinic and he kept a chart of her fertile days and those were the days that, in the words of Celie from Purple, he climbed on top of her and did his business.

Once they had gotten married, Caliphs made her quit her job. He said it did not look right for a man of his caliber to have a working wife, so she stayed home and spent Caliphs' money. One day when she was having the deck remodeled, the handyman that was working on the house knocked on the door and asked for a cold glass of water. Before she knew it, she was giving him more than a glass of water on a weekly basis. Five months after she started this affair, she started not feeling like herself and when she went to the doctor, she found out that she was two months pregnant. At first, she was excited thinking that this was the heir to the Winfield Dynasty.

For a fleeting moment, she thought of the possibility that it might be the handyman's baby. Caliphs was so excited when he found that Theresa was pregnant and he was ecstatic when he discovered that it was a boy.

Theresa went into labor two months early and Charles was born weighing three pounds. He was born with a heart defect and at one month old, he needed surgery. In the middle of the surgery, he started to lose blood and needed a blood transfusion. The doctors had told Caliphs and Theresa when a baby is that young and fragile they usually like to take the blood from the mother or the father. When they tested both parents' blood, they were both O positive so either one of them should have been able to donate, but when they tested Charles, his blood type was AB so there was no way that Caliphs could have been Charles' father.

Caliphs was devastated when he found out and paid off the doctors so their secret would never leave the hospital.

"How could you cheat on me and wind up pregnant when you know how bad I wanted a baby boy? You disgust me. By the way, who is this bastard's father?"

"I don't know."

"How many men has it been? You can take the whore out of the whorehouse, but you can't take the whore out of the woman." From that day on, Caliphs and Theresa had separate bedrooms and he never touched her again.

Two years later, Theresa found out that she was pregnant again. She considered having an abortion, but had decided against it and had the baby. When Caliphs found out that she was pregnant, he was livid and threatened to throw her and both of her bastard children out.

"Can you imagine what your father would do if he found out your dirty little secret? What would all of your lawyer buddies think? I am sure that Bishop Kelley would love to find out that the man that won the Prelate seat from him practices sins that are against the church rules," she taunted. "Now, we will continue to keep each other's secrets, won't we dear?"

They pretty much led separate lives. Caliphs spent most of his time at the law firm or at the church. He was rarely at home and Theresa spent her days between sleeping with other men and shopping at all the high-end stores.

One day, Caliphs came home early from a business trip and caught Teresa and her lover in the bed together. Caliphs told the handyman, "You are fired! Get out of my house!"

"It will not be that easy to get rid of me. I need to stay around so I can see my two children grow up."

"Theresa, you got pregnant by the hired help?" Caliphs paid the handyman a million dollars to go away and stay away from his wife and his children.

Lady Theresa opened her eyes and remembered she was at the hospital and that her only son was dying or basically already dead. She thought about that awful day when she should have finally walked away from Caliphs and all his secrets.

One night, Lady Theresa could not sleep and decided to check on the children. When she went in Charles' room she found Caliphs standing over Charles with his pants down committing an unthinkable act. Charles was crying softly and Caliphs was saying, "You know what Daddy likes."

Theresa ran into the room screaming. "What in the heck are you doing to my child?"

Caliphs looked up, pulled up his pants, and ran out of the room crying. Theresa held Charles. "Did Caliphs make you do anything else?"

"No, he just put his peepee in my mouth."

Theresa went to Caliphs. "If you ever touch my child again, jail will be too good for you and in hell will you open your eyes."

A couple of years after was when Charles started to act effeminate and she took out all her aggravation on Charlisa who reminded her of her past.

Dr. Stein and Dr. Wand came in to the family room and startled her out of her nightmare.

"Hello, my name Is Dr. Wand. How are you this afternoon?"

"As well as can be expected," Lady Theresa said.

"I am sorry, but my test results are the same as Dr. Stein's. There is no brain activity."

Caliphs walked over to Lady Theresa and attempted to put his hand on her back, but she pulled away. Charlisa came back into the room and saw her mother crying. She

TIME TO BREAK THE BARRIER

went over to her mother and attempted to console her, but her mother pulled away.

"Can I be there when you pull the plug?" Lady Theresa asked quietly.

"After we remove the plug, then you can come in the room and stay with him."

Lady Theresa looked at Caliphs and said, "When I get back to the house, please don't be there by the time I leave this hospital. I don't want to see any sign of any of your belongings." Just as they were getting ready to leave the room, a man ran into the room.

"Excuse me, sir, this room is only for immediate family," the doctor stated.

"I'm no stranger. That's my son lying in there and I want to know what's going on."

"Charles, I told you not to come here."

"I am tired of listening to you. Your money is not everything. I allowed you to keep me away from my family long enough."

Charlisa found herself getting dizzy and when she woke up, she was hooked up to an IV. The doctors came in to talk to her.

"You're dehydrated, your potassium levels are extremely high, and your heartbeat is irregular. All these symptoms are characteristic of someone who is bulimic. Do you eat and purge afterwards?

Charlisa nodded her head yes and started to cry.

"If you would like, you can take the IV pole and go into your brother's room. They pulled the plug and he is barely breathing on his own."

Charlisa got off the hospital bed and pulled the IV pole down the hall. When she got to the room, her mother was lying over her brother on the bed and the man that claimed to be her father was staring out the window. Charlisa walked over to her brother's bed. "Charles, I am going to miss you. I love you and..." Charlisa started to cry hysterically.

After about fifteen minutes, Charles took his last breath and Charlisa was standing on one side holding his hand. Lady Theresa was still lying across Charles and she was crying and talking to him.

"I am so sorry that I was a terrible mother and I tried to make it up to you, but I never could. Charles, I know that it is too late, but I want to apologize to you from the depths of my soul for how my actions destroyed you and Charlisa. I caused you tremendous hurt and pain. I made some decisions that were selfish. When I saw that Caliphs was hurting you, I thought I was protecting you in some sick, twisted way, but I did not leave him. You thought everything was your fault, but you were the victim. You have every right to hate me. There are just so many things that you do not understand. I thought that I could run away from my past, but my future was being held prisoner by my past. I was filled with darkness and I wanted to escape it. I allowed my past to define who I was by running from it. I ruined the lives of the only people that I loved in my limited capacity to love anybody, because I never learned how to love myself."

She turned to Charlisa who was looking at her mother with disbelief. "Charlisa, I am so sorry for how I treated you. I hated you because you reminded me of my past. There are so many things that you do not know about me. Everything you see now is made up. My name is not even Theresa. One day I will tell you everything, but this is enough for now. I should deal with your brother's death and where do we go from here? By me running away from my past, I was pushing you into overeating and overachieving, trying to fit into the mold that I tried to make for you. There are so many secrets in this family that you do not know about. The love of money fueled me and the fear of going back to the hell that I came from. The first thing that I want to do is to admit that Caliphs is not your real father. Charles is your biological father. Many years ago, Caliphs paid him off to go away and over the years, he resented me because I deprived him of his family. I have stayed in contact with him over the years by sending him school pictures. I did not want to destroy the picture that Caliphs and I had painted, but now I see it was never worth it."

Charlisa looked over at Charles and he was silently sobbing. The nurse came in the room. "You have a few more minutes before we have to take the body to the morgue."

Charlisa walked slowly back to her room and sat on the bed. She was still crying as she looked at the IV in her arm and she thought to herself, 'I never thought my life would end up like this.'

As she was thinking to herself, the nurse came in and said, "I am here to take your IV off, and in a few minutes, you can go home when I come back with your discharge papers. The doctor wants you to see your primary doctor immediately."

As Charlisa was walking out of her room, she ran straight into her mother and they all walked out of the hospital and went their separate ways. For the first time in days, Charlisa jumped into her car. She was tired and confused. Before she pulled out of the parking garage, she pulled out her cell phone to check her messages and to start the horrible task of calling Charles' friends to let them know that he died.

Charlisa looked at her phone and saw that David had left her another message. He said, "I was waiting for you to call me. I guess you are not interested."

Charlisa thought over the events of today of how her mother's past had destroyed their family and her mother's chance of happiness. She wanted to break the barriers to love in her life. She admitted that she must first learn to love herself and realized that her past experiences had hardened her heart, and she had thrown away any dreams of really being happy and finding her Beau. She was tired of the façade. She was sick of being a public success, but a private failure. She pretended in front of people that she was happy, but she wasn't. She had turned to food for comfort. She ate when she was happy and when she was sad. She tried to make people love her that did not love themselves. It was a generational curse, a curse that would be broken with her. She did not want to feel that emotional pain, but she knew that she would be able to live through it.

"It is time for me to get real with myself," Charlisa thought. "I have to stop with this self-hatred." She said over and over, "I am wonderful and marvelously made. I will lose this weight in a healthy way. I will go to counseling and seek spiritual guidance. I am going to move out of my comfort zone and stop believing in the same-old-same-old, but I am going to try something new. I am going to slowly break down all the walls that I had built to protect myself because they did not work. I will stop all my acts of self-sabotage."

Charlisa looked at herself in the mirror and said, "I am sorry that Charles had to die for me to be free, but I will not let Charles' death be in vain. I will love myself and accept all the many parts of me. I do not care from this minute on what people think about me. I will no longer look to satisfy others and try to make people accept me. I will not allow anybody to hurt me again. I will not allow people, places, or things to kill my dreams. There has been too much heartache in my life as I tried to take people with me who were just not meant to go where I am going. I will not be a prisoner anymore. I am moving forward, not looking backwards. I cannot change the events of my past. In the words of Patti Labelle, "I'm feeling good from my head to my shoes. I know where I am going and I know what to do. I tidied up my point of view, I got a new attitude."

Charlisa put the car into drive and rolled down the window to allow the wind to blow. She turned on the radio and instead of going home, even though she knew that she needed a shower, she wanted to go to Jones Beach to sit by the water and just think over her life and the new things that she had just affirmed in her life. Charlisa knew that starting over again was not going to be easy, but she knew that it was going to be worth it. The first thing that she was going to do was to quit her job at the law firm. She did not know what tomorrow held for her, but she knew that she no longer wanted to work at the firm. She wanted to start an organization for children and adults who have been physically and emotionally abused. She wanted to name it 'No Longer Victims but Overcomers.'

As she sat by the water, she looked down and saw David's number and decided that the first step in the rest of her life was to make that call. As she dialed the number, she looked up and saw a dove flying overhead. "This is a sign that I am on the right track to healing," she thought. "I do not need a man to complete me. My life is complete and I am on the way to loving me so I am not going to make any permanent decisions while I am still in this temporary state, but let's see where this is going." She dialed the number and on the third ring, David answered.

"Hello, this is Charlisa."

"I have been waiting for you to call."

"I wasn't going to call because you said that you are not into heavy woman."

"No, I said I don't usually date BBWs, but there's something about you that made me want to know you better. I am not looking at the outward appearance because the outward can change. I want to know your heart."

"I had a really rough week. I just need someone to talk to right now. I am just looking for a friend."

"I will be your friend. We are not in rush. Let's just take it one day at a time and get to know each other."

"I am going to be busy for the next few months, but I will not forget your number and I am going to give you my number."

"I will be waiting. I believe that it's time for both of us to break some barriers in our lives. Good night, beautiful."

"Good night," Charlisa replied before looking up towards the sky. "Thank you, Jesus."

"Small World"

By

Tukisha M. Knox

Tukisha M. Knox, a native of New York, currently resides in New Jersey with her husband, two children and puppy. She is an inspiring writer who divides her time working in the nonprofit sector and being an entrepreneur and brand ambassador. Small World is her first piece of work.

Dedication

I dedicate this short story to women who have experienced love, be it their first love, dangerous love, crazy love or unconditional love. I've loved and learned that the most important love is self-love.

CHAPTER 1

CAMILLE

Camille sat alone in her living room, sipping green tea. The melody of a slow love song bellowed in the background. Her legs had grown tiresome of pacing the floor anticipating Dave's return. She sat and wondered where and what he was doing. She awoke earlier to an empty bed and was resigned yet again to breakfast alone. Camille felt a surge of anger fill her body. Things had been going so well with Dave. She had finally found happiness after one of the most tumultuous years of her life, and he was truly fucking it up.

Camille had been dating Dave for a little over a year now. She met him at her gym, Platinum Fitness. She had just arrived to take her Wednesday night Cardio Funk class, and he was finishing up the repair of a broken glass in one of the studios. She could feel his eyes on her backside as she sashayed across the room. The class began to fill up and he quickly made his exit.

Camille was a pretty girl; she stood about five feet four, one hundred and fifty pounds, mostly booty. She had the complexion of a diet peach Snapple, with medium length hair and a smile that was simply irresistible.

It was approaching eight o'clock in the evening and getting dark out. Daylight savings time made the day seem so much longer. Camille tried Dave's cell and, just as expected, the call went straight to voicemail. She tossed her cell phone on the sofa, refusing to leave any more messages; eight was enough.

Camille turned out the lights in the house and retreated to her bedroom. She wasn't ready to go to sleep, but she needed to get her mind off of Dave. She stepped out of her clothes, put on her favorite nightshirt, and went to retrieve her cell phone from the living room. She pressed the home button to see if she had any missed calls or text messages. Beep, Beep, beep. She looked down to see that there were none and that her battery was at eight percent. Before returning to the bedroom, she peeked through the slightly opened window blind, hoping she would see Dave pulling into the driveway.

Camille connected her cell to the charger and stretched out across her queen size bed. She reached over to her clock radio on her nightstand and hit the alarm which was set for six in the morning.

Camille closed her eyes and imagined the perfect ending to her and Dave's conflict. He would come in the door with her favorite weekend dinner, fish and chips with two slices of wheat bread from Famous on 145th and St. Nicholas in Harlem. He would kiss her and let her know that his phone died while he was out clearing his head. She'd understand; she wasn't clingy, just a bit insecure.

Camille got caught up in her daydream for fifteen minutes, running different scenarios in her head. She picked up her now fully charged phone and dialed up her right-hand girl.

"What's up, girl?" chimed the voice on the other end.

"I give up," exclaimed Camille into the phone.

"What happened now?" said Kelli

"I cannot win for losing; something has got to give," Camille replied. "I mean, really, why do I keep getting the short end of the stick?"

"This man leaves out before I even wake up and he's not back yet. It's going on eight o'clock now, and he hasn't even called."

Kelli tried to console her friend. "Calm down. I'm sure he has a reason," said Kelli. "Maybe his phone is dead?"

"Just wait till he gets in here. It's on," said Camille.

"Don't do anything crazy. Be easy," said Kelli.

Camille was no stranger to drama in her life. Only two years ago, she had divorced her husband, Sean, after ten years of marriage. They had been high school sweethearts and each other's first true love. They were young when they married and couldn't handle the commitment once it was official. Somehow, that piece of paper changed everything. They remained friends, but tried their best to keep their distance from each other whenever they were involved in relationships.

"Guess where we are going on the 24th?" said Camille into the phone while swaying her head from side to side to the music playing in her head.

"Where are *we* going?" said Kelli.

"To M-S-G," she sang into the phone.

"Say word?" said Kelli.

"Word! You, Caprise, Troi and I are going. I just won four front row tickets on the radio to see Anthony Hamilton, Joe, and my future husband, Maxwell.

"Say word," said Kelli.

"Word," she said.

"You are too fucking lucky. Every time I turn around, you winning something. I love Joe. What am I going to wear? What are you wearing?" Kelli was asking twenty-one questions in rapid speed.

"I just won the tickets. I haven't thought about it yet, damn," Camille retorted. Camille heard a brief beep on the line. "Hold on, I got another call," she told Kelli.

"Hello?" said Camille into the speaker.

"Hey, stranger," chimed the voice on the other end.

"Hey, I'm on the other line with Kelli. Hold on."

"Kelli, that's Dave on the other line. Let me hear what he has to say. I'll call you back later. Do me a favor, call Caprise and tell her the good news."

"Alight girl," said Kelli. "I'll talk to you later and be nice."

"Whatever," Camille replied.

Chapter 2

Camille, Caprise, and Kelli arrived at the Garden an hour before the eight pm show was set to start. They were looking extra fine that night, so they decided to kill some time taking pictures. Just as Caprise was about to snap the picture, some chick photobombed the picture.

Kelli was about to whip out a can of whip ass when she recognized the chick was Troi.

"What are you doing here?" said Camille.

Troi had told the girls that she had a prior engagement and she would catch up with them the following night.

"Well, there was a change in plans," said Troi.

"Kyle, meet my crazy ass friends. They are like sisters to me. Camille, Kelli, and Caprise." After introducing her girls to her new boo, she and Kyle went off and weren't seen again for the rest of the night.

Troi was the uninhibited one of the group. She changed men like she changed her underwear. She longed for a commitment, but never stayed with a man long enough to get to know him.

Troi needed to realize that she didn't make the best decisions when it came to her love interests. She had been in every type of relationship imaginable. She fell in love fast, and she loved hard.

Maxwell did his thing that night. His caramel skin and sexy voice were turning all the women on. When he sang one of his first hits, "Let the cops come knocking," the crowd went crazy. Anthony Hamilton had women swinging their hands from side to side as he belted out "Charlene." Joe didn't even have to sing. As soon as he appeared on stage, the ladies began chanting his name. He opened with "Things your man won't do."

Camille kept shouting over and over, "You can get it, Joe, you can definitely get it."

CHAPTER 3

TROI

"Where did you go last night, heifer?" asked Caprise.

"Girl, you will never believe what happened," stated Troi.

"Kyle and I didn't even get to see the show," said Troi with a hint of guilt in her voice.

"Do tell, do tell, what happened?" Caprise inquired.

"Well, if you must know." Troi giggled a bit.

"I must," said Caprise as a matter of fact.

"Kyle ran into a friend of his who had backstage access. We heard the show, but was too busy to see it. We found an empty room and decided to get better acquainted with each other. We kissed lightly at first, then Kyle's hand moved slowly under my shirt. It was on from there," said Troi. Caprise could hear her grinning from ear to ear through the phone.

Troi was a petite woman. A size four at the most, but with a size fourteen personality. She spoke her mind and lived life on the edge compared to her friends.

"What else did you do?"

"Nothing," said Troi innocently, but not fooling Caprise one bit.

"I don't believe you. Did you give him some cake?" Caprise asked.

That was the girls' code for going all the way. They had been using the word cake for years, even as adults. Vagina sounded so nasty, and coochie was a bit juvenile. Cake was nice and sweet, and so it became another name for the goodies.

"No, I just let him taste the frosting a bit." Troi could barely contain her laughter.

"Un, un, un," said Caprise as she shook her head. "You're too much for me, Ms. Thang."

In that instant, Troi had lied to her sister friend. At the time, she wasn't ashamed, but now that she was telling the story, she felt ashamed that she had once again allowed lust to get the best of her. No one had to know the details anyway. It would be between her and God. She used to share all of her intimate and personal secrets with her girls, but they were getting older, and she didn't want to be judged.

Troi had struggled to keep her composure, but once Kyle's fingertips grazed her breast, she had to go with the flow. Her breast was the most sensitive spot on her body. She tingled within and once he slipped his fingers underneath her skirt and along the crotch of her underwear, her secret was out. He had turned her on, and the sticky film on his fingers told him so. He held his hand up to his nose and inhaled deeply.

In between kisses and nibbles, Kyle whispered, "I love the scent of a woman and the taste too." Before Troi realized what was happening, Kyle had taken a seat on the step below her and had his head beneath her skirt. Minutes later, he had her skirt up around her waist and her legs wrapped around his midsection. He entered her ever so gently, and she seemed to be floating on air. Sweat trickled down Kyle's temples and Troi's do was done when they finished. Once out of the arena and in Kyle's Mercedes truck, they were all over each other again. Kyle reached for a condom inside the glove department and they went another round.

CHAPTER 4

CAPRISE

After the show, they all went to Cove up in Harlem for a nightcap. By two am, everyone was in their cars waving goodnight.

Caprise was ready to get back to Joe. They had been through two very rocky years and were finally getting their marriage back on track. They had both made mistakes in the past and were trying to move forward.

After finding out that Joe was seeing a younger woman, Caprise decided to get revenge. Toni was the name of the chick he was seeing. She was a sophomore in college, still living with her parents, and Joe was playing sugar daddy. At first he denied it, but there was too much evidence. Caprise found notes to him from her in their car and receipts for items she didn't own from stores she didn't shop at. She began to save phone numbers on his cell phone bills. She put two and two together, but it all was confirmed when she found pictures of Toni in his briefcase. In a fury, she tore them up and told him that she was leaving. She even called Toni up and told her that she could have the sorry bastard. She claimed that she never knew anything about Caprise, but she knew it was a lie. Caprise told the heifer and her mother that she knew where they lived and that if she found out that she was still keeping in contact with Joe that she was going to come to her house and personally kick her ass. Soon after, the calls stopped.

The last few months with Joe were rocky, but somehow Caprise was optimistic. She let the unanswered phone calls to Joe go without saying much. She was trying to let him breathe. Little did she know Toni was still in the picture.

Joe had taken Toni under his wing just the year prior. He loved a damsel in distress. Toni herself didn't threaten Caprise, just what she represented. Joe played it cool but as the saying goes, *what happens in the dark eventually comes to light.*

The red light flickered and instantly the message icon appeared. Caprise thought to herself, 'Should I look—why not?' She picked up Joe's phone and pressed the button to read the message. Slowly, the words scrolled across the screen and Caprise's blood began to boil. She read the words *Love you Always, Toni.* She instantly wanted to fight. Caprise didn't play when it came to her man. This bitch Toni was getting out of hand.

Joe denied knowing anything about the message. Why Toni had to decided to text him now, out of the blue, was unbeknownst to him. He didn't have a clue.

Caprise should have been a private eye because her mind went into overdrive when she wanted answers. This was not the end of it. She was determined to find out what was really going on.

The next day, while on her lunch break Caprise stopped at an Internet café she had passed on several occasions. She bought herself a vanilla Chai tea, found a computer in the back, and commenced to doing some research.

Hmmm. She thought to herself, *what would her password be?* Toni's, that is. *Let's see, she's young and doesn't know any better. I bet it's her birthday...no, too simple. I bet it's her most prized possession.*

Caprise typed in the letters N-I-N-A. Jackpot! *So, predictable, these young girls.* She said to herself, *I'm in.* Joe's work and cell numbers were all up and down the pages.

Dates, times, minutes, incoming mostly, but outgoing too. There it was in black and white.

Caprise's heart was racing again, and rage was slowly overwhelming her. She wanted to forget work, go and get her car, and drive straight to the bitch's house and drop her. Caprise wasn't the fighting type, but at this moment in time, she was ready for whatever. She proceeded to print every page.

CHAPTER 5

KELLI

Kelli was the undercover bad girl of the group. She had everything going for her. She had graduated from college, had a nice home, a good man, and was about to start her own business. She and Barry were in the longest engagement ever...six long years.

Barry was a Java-colored brother with buns of steel. Barry had been the most popular guy in high school. He was voted most likely to succeed and the finest guy in the entire senior class. Barry hadn't lost his looks or his physique. They met at the Black Expo in Atlanta. Kelli had visited almost every cubicle in the area and was about to leave when their eyes met.

He examined her from head to toe. She wore her hair in a short, reddish bob cut. She had on one of her best Donna Karan suits. He ran his eyes the length of her silky stocking legs right down to the size seven mocha pumps she wore from David & Jones. Kelli could wear some clothes. She had champagne taste and the money to back it up.

Kelli enjoyed being with Barry because he was an old-fashioned kind of guy. He still believed in chivalry and knew how to treat a woman. This was due to his southern background. He was born and raised in Richmond Virginia and had come to New York to study at NYU. At first, their relationship seemed like something out of a storybook. They had everything that a couple could ask for—communication, trust, and loyalty—but Kelli felt that something was missing. She felt Barry was the man she wanted to marry, but lately she wasn't so sure.

CHAPTER 6

CAMILLE

"Camille, baby. What would you say if I told you that I wanted you to spend the Fourth of July with me?"

"Well, Dave, you know that the girls and I made plans to go to the Bahamas that weekend. Kelli went through a lot to set this trip up, plus I already put down my deposit."

While Dave and Camille were on the outs, she had started to go out with her girlfriends more. She had decided to start living and stop dwelling on her trivial relationships with men.

"What about letting me down?" Dave asked. "Why can't you ever sacrifice for me? It's always about your girls."

"Who's more important anyway? The girls or me?" he continued to complain.

Camille struggled with her feelings while listening to Dave. "Please don't make me choose."

"I'm always here for you. Why are you being so selfish? When you want to go somewhere, you just bounce."

Camille was starting to tear up. She hated when she cried during an argument. She always felt like she was showing a sign of weakness. She was just so damn frustrated with Dave's antics.

"Besides, I made these plans when you went AWOL on me. Now you're back and I'm supposed to drop everything?"

"Yes," Dave responded. "I should come before anyone else."

"Look, this getaway is paid for already, and I can't get a refund."

TIME TO BREAK THE BARRIER

CHAPTER 7

TROI

After the second round, Troi and Kyle exchanged numbers and made plans to hook up again. Two days had passed, and Troi still hadn't heard from Kyle.

"Should I leave another message, you guys?"

"Yeah," said Camille.

"Hell no," said Sinclair. "Let him call you."

"You two are not helping. Yes or no?"

"Call him," said Camille. "Why shouldn't you call him? Besides, maybe he lost your number."

Sinclair retorted, "No, no, no. You don't have sex with someone twice in the same night and just lose her number." Sinclair was pissed off for Troi. "What type of shit is that? You don't forget to call someone who you just knocked boots with."

"Yes, you do if that someone gave it up on the first date," said Camille. "You know what Troi? You really are a whore."

"F you, Camille. I'm not no whore. It just happened, and I did use protection. Oh shit!"

"What?" said Camille.

"I used protection in his car, but not in the staircase. I can't believe it. I am such an idiot. I swear I'm never drinking again."

"You can't be serious," said Sinclair with disdain.

"Are you crazy? How could you be so irresponsible?" Camille asked.

"Let me get off this phone before my shit gets turned off," said Sinclair. "Messing with you two, my bill will be sky high."

Camille replied, "Okay girl, I'll talk to you tomorrow and you, Troi, I'll see you tomorrow."

Troi hung up and tried calling Kyle. Again and again, she got his machine. "Hi, this is Kyle. Leave a message."

"Hey sweetie, this is Troi, give me a call." She hung up and tears came to her eyes. She knew that she had made the biggest mistake of her life. She realized that she would probably never see him again.

CHAPTER 8

CAPRISE

Joe continued to deny every accusation that Caprise hit him with. He swore there was no one else, but she could see in his eyes that he was just telling her lies. The last straw was when Joe, who had never ever spent the night away from home, went away for the weekend. He wouldn't give Caprise any details about his trip, not even where he was going, who he was going with, or for how long he would be gone.

Joe had been making plans. Toni had finally broken him down. She had begged for many weeks to go away for just a weekend. She was on vacation and couldn't enjoy it because Joe only had a few hours a week to spend with her. She tried to keep busy by seeing Kelli, but that's not who she really wanted to spend her time with.

Joe had plenty of friends, but they were all married or in long term relationships. Caprise couldn't think of anyone he'd go away with except his pretty young thing and there was nothing she could do about it. She had no more tears.

Chapter 9

TROI

"What do you see? A plus or a minus?"

"Wait a minute, will you? It's only been thirty seconds. We have to wait two minutes," said Kelli.

"I can't take this waiting. I don't even know why I wasted my money on that stupid test. I already know what the answer is. I haven't had my period in two months. I just know that I'm pregnant."

"You sure are, girl. I'm sorry, Troi."

"Don't be, Kel. I knew the consequences and I took the risk anyway."

"So, what are you going to do?"

"I don't know yet."

CHAPTER 10

SINCLAIR

"Hey girl, it's me. Give me a ring when you get in, I got news." Sinclair had been seeing this guy for a month now, and things were starting to heat up.

Later that night, after a long tedious day, Camille finally sat in her favorite chair with a freshly brewed cup of tea and called Sinclair.

"What's this I hear of news?" said Camille. "And how long have you had it?"

"Shut up, girl. It's new news. Anyway, I met this guy. He's from your part of town. Anyway, his name is Banks and he's a correctional officer. He is fine, girl, and has a heart of gold."

"Awwh, Sinclair gotta boo. I'm happy for you," said Camille. "Now you have someone to keep you company out there in Philly. Especially since you don't visit us anymore."

"You know how it is," Sinclair responded. "I'm always doing overtime and a weekend just isn't enough time to really relax, especially when you count traveling time."

"True," said Camille. "But you could come on a four-day weekend sometimes."

"Okay, I'll try." Sinclair was a New Yorker like the rest of them, but she relocated to Philly right after graduation from high school. Her job was moving to Philly, so she left. She didn't have any children or a man, so there wasn't any reason for her to stay.

CHAPTER 11

TROI

"Excuse me, I have an appointment with Dr. McIntyre for 11:30."

"Yes, please fill out the forms on the clipboard and return them to me with your insurance card and I will check you in."

Troi followed the receptionist's instructions and returned the clipboard along with her insurance card. The slender woman looked over the forms, making sure that Troi had signed in all the appropriate spaces, then handed Troi her insurance card.

"Ok, Ms. Majors," said the nurse. "Have a seat. The doctor will be with you shortly."

After her appointment, Troi looked up at the clock which now said 12:10. She picked up her coat and purse and headed for the elevator. She felt like she was about to cry. She felt the tears start to well up. She held her head up to the ceiling to keep the tears from falling and said a prayer to God. "You've blessed me once more with the gift of life and this time I am ready." She turned to her left where the letters EXIT glowed a bright red. She raced down three flights of stairs and didn't look back.

Several years earlier, while a freshman in high school, Troi had gotten pregnant. She hid the pregnancy from her family and got an abortion. At the time, she was too young to be a mother, but so in love that she almost kept the baby. This time around she was emotionally and financially ready. She had made a mistake, but was determined to turn it into a blessing.

"Kelli, would you do me the honor of being the godmother of my child?" asked Troi.

"Are you kidding me? I would love to," said Kelli. "So, how far along are you?"

"Eleven weeks," said Troi.

"Any word on Kyle?"

"Not a word. The sad thing about it is that I don't even know his last name. I've prepared myself to raise this baby by myself anyway, so it really doesn't matter."

CHAPTER 12

CAMILLE

"Are you still upset with me?" Dave asked Camille.

"No, I guess one day won't kill me. I'm sorry for over reacting, but baby, I feel like I'm losing you. I don't know why I get so jealous."

"Oh, come here honey, I'm not going anywhere."

The two snuggled a bit then headed for the bedroom where they made love.

In the morning, they got up, went for their daily jog, then had breakfast together at their favorite diner. Dave headed off to work and Camille to Kelli's house. They always hung out together on Sundays to discuss the events of the past week.

"Congratulations! I hear you're going to be a godmother."

"Yeah, Troi decided to keep the baby. Maybe this will slow her down."

"So how are you and Barry doing?" asked Camille.

"We're okay. Things could be better, though."

Kelli's feelings for Barry were slowly changing. They did less and less together. Actually, Kelli was seeing someone else.

"Barry seems like the perfect match for you, girl. Don't give up so easily."

"I'm trying, but he doesn't seem interested. We haven't had sex in months. That's a record for us. Oh well, that's another story," said Camille. "Enough about my problems. What's up with Caprise?"

"I talked to her the other day. She seemed fine. Let's give her a call."

"Bet."

The three of them decided to go catch a matinee at the concourse.

"I hear this movie is the bomb," said Caprise.

"You always say that," said Kelli. "Remember when you convinced us to go see that Austin Powers crap? You said that was the bomb, and it was wick, wick, wack. You're lucky it was your turn to pay. Troi is going to be pissed that we didn't invite her. Her ass is probably asleep anyway. Now that she's pregnant, she sleeps longer than usual. We'll go see her after the movie. Let's take her some vanilla wafers," said Kelli. "She loves them."

Chapter 13

KELLI

"Kelli, this is T. Meet me at Mekka's tonight at eight. I need to see you."

Kelli replayed the message three times, then erased it. "What should I tell Barry and what am I going to wear?" she thought to herself. "I know, I'll wear my baby blue halter-top with my black shirt and my baby blue sandals. Yeah, Camille's baby blue coach tote bag would go perfect with that. Perfect. Now what do I tell Barry?"

At that moment, Kelli's phone rang and it was Barry. "Hello."

"Hi baby."

"I have bad news. I won't be able to see you tonight. Troi's feeling a little down, so the girls and I are going over to her house to cheer her up. I might stay over so I'll see you tomorrow, okay?"

Barry was disappointed, but he never interfered with Kelli's plans. "Okay, baby, love you."

Kelli plugged in the hot curler while she did her makeup. Afterwards she touched up her hair, grabbed her sweater, and was out the door.

"Hi, T."

"I'm glad that you called."

"So am I. You look stunning. I wasn't sure that you would be able to make it."

"Neither was I, but I really wanted to see you. We've been spending a lot of time together recently and I really feel comfortable around you. I think about you when I'm at work, home, and even when I'm with Barry. I wish we didn't have to sneak around, but no one would understand. I told my girlfriends that I was seeing someone other than Barry, but I didn't get specific."

"It's cool. When you're ready."

After dinner and a few drinks, they went back to T's house. After they both slipped into something more comfortable, T turned the lights low and put on some music. Maxwell bellowed in the background as T messaged Kelli's shoulders. Kelli began to moan and soon her nightie was off of her shoulders and around her waist.

"Take it all the way off and your panties too," said T.

Kelli did as told and lay on the sofa. T spread Kelli's legs and was positioned directly opposite her navel. T kissed her navel and the surrounding area until she found the mark. Kelli couldn't remember ever feeling the way she felt when she was with T. She hadn't had sex in almost a month and it was about time she released some stress. She was also becoming emotionally attached to T. How would she explain her feelings to her friends and how would they react? She knew she was wrong for cheating on Barry, but it didn't feel so wrong because she was with another woman. She couldn't help the way she felt. Everyone would have to understand.

CHAPTER 14

CAMILLE

"You bastard! How dare you hit me! You know what? I've had enough of this bullshit. I want you to leave! Get out! Get out!"

"I'm sorry. Camille, I'm sorry. You know I love you. I just get crazy sometimes. Please don't leave me."

"Hell no, motherfucker, you get your shit and you get out now before I call the police."

"Alright, alright, I'm going. You need time to clear your head and realize that you're making a mistake. I'll be at my mom's."

"I don't give a shit where you'll be. I hate you so much right now!" Camille screamed with tears running down her face.

*****

"Where the fuck is everybody?"

"Calm down, Camille," said Sinclair into the phone. "Caprise and Joe went to the Poconos. Troi is here with Kelli and me."

"Well, I need you guys right now. Dave and I just had a big fight and I don't know what to do. I can't believe it. A man has never hit me. Dave has serious problems and until he can work them out, I can't be with him anymore. You know what? I will call you guys later. I need some air."

"Wait, wait Camille, don't hang up. We..." Click, the phone went dead.

"Sean, it's Mil, can I come over?"

"Sure, what happened?"

"I'll tell you when I get there," said Camille. "I'm jumping in a cab. Be there in fifteen." Camille hung up the phone, grabbed her bag, and locked the door behind her.

She and Sean had separated on good terms. They were both having problems committing to each other and rather than getting a divorce, they decided to separate for a while. They both realized that they had married too young. They remained friends and could still talk to each other amicably.

Camille was still in tears when she arrived at Sean's house. He held her close and they reminisced about old times.

"Do you remember the first time I saw you cry? You were so beautiful even with big, red, puffy eyes. I held you and you hugged me so tight like I was your protector from the world. Why is it that we get along so well apart and fight when we are together? I love you so much, Camille. I see women here and there, but no one compares to you."

"Don't just be saying these things to get back with me, Sean," said Camille with a suspicious eye.

"To tell you the truth, Camille, I've always hoped that some jerk would send you back into my arms. Everything is just the way you left it, Mil." He was using his pet name for Camille purposely. "The door is open whenever you want to come home. Tonight, I'll sleep on the couch. You get some rest and we'll talk in the morning."

"Thanks Sean, you were always a great provider. Good night."

CHAPTER 15

SINCLAIR

"Hey ladies," said Sinclair into the phone.

"Hey," they all shouted in unison.

"What's new?" said Camille.

"When you coming to New York?" asked Kelli.

"I'm getting married," said Sinclair.

"You're what?" questioned Camille with excitement in her voice.

"I said I'm getting married!"

"Well damn, Sin, when did you get engaged? Are you pregnant?" asked Caprise.

"No, I am not pregnant," said Sinclair. "But I have found the man of my dreams and I'm getting married!"

CHAPTER 16

CAMILLE

Sean thought about Camille more since she spent the night with him. He had been seeing several women on the regular, but no one to bring home to mama. He hadn't loved anyone the way he loved Camille. He wanted to be with her again, but only when he was positively sure that he was ready to settle down. Separating from her was the hardest thing he ever had to do and he didn't want to lose her twice.

Camille thought about how safe she felt when she was in Sean's arms. They had a special love for each other. No matter who each of them were with at the time, there was always a place in their hearts that belonged to the other.

"Hey, Mil, I really enjoyed having you over. I'm just checking on you. Give me a call when you get in." Camille played the message over and over and thought about when they first met several years ago.

They were both at a party of a mutual friend and when Bobby Brown's smash hit "Tenderoni" played, he asked her to dance. They danced to that song and to every song that played for the rest of the night. Couples actually danced to slow songs at parties back then. Once the party was over and the lights went up, Camille disappeared.

Sean called everyone he knew and asked if they knew Camille. It took almost a month, but finally he found a girl who dated a guy who knew a girl that went to school with Camille. Phone calls were made, messages were relayed, and finally he was able to get her number and gave her a call.

"Hello, this message is for the beautiful woman whom I danced all night with and then vanished on me. My name is Sean and I would like to see you again. My number is 555-6301. I'll be waiting for your call."

Camille had replayed that message repeatedly. "So, his name is Sean," she said to herself. "I wonder if he spells it like Jay Z or Puffy. Either way, I can't believe he got my number, but I'm glad he did. I'll call him tomorrow," she continued to talk to herself. "I'll let him sweat a little."

The next day, she took a deep breath and after practicing her sexy voice in the bathroom mirror, she picked up the receiver and began to dial. Her palms were sweaty and her heart began to race. Slowly she hit the buttons with her thumb 5-5-5... "Maybe it's too early. Not everyone gets up early on Saturdays. Hell, I better do it now before I chicken out." She clicked the button to get a dial tone again and dialed quickly this time before she could change her mind. 5-5-5-6-3-0-1. *The phone rang once, twice, then the sexiest voice she had ever heard answered.*

"Hello?"

"Hey there, Mr. Private Eye," Camille said in her rehearsed sexy voice.

"Well, well, well. I thought you'd never call."

"What makes you say that?" *Camille was puzzled. He had just left a message for her with his phone number only two days ago.*

"It took you over twenty-four hours to call. I said that I'd be waiting."

Camille's heart fluttered at his honesty. "You were? I'm sorry," *she said in her little girl angel voice.*

"Don't worry," *said Sean.* "You can make it up to me by going to dinner with me."

"How about tonight?"

"Tonight is fine."

Camille and Sean exchanged information and decided where to meet up. They went out that night and were inseparable after that night. Sean was Camille's first love and she meant the world to him.

Camille picked up the phone and called Sean. He answered on the first ring.

"Hey, Sean, it's me."

"Hey, Mil, what's up?"

"How about dinner tonight, on me?"

"Tonight is fine. I'll pick you up at eight."

"Okay, see you then."

CHAPTER 17

KELLI

"Hey, sexy, could we spend the night alone tonight, just you and me?"

"Sure, I'm not going anywhere," said Kelli.

"How about we rent a movie and snuggle up?" suggested Barry.

"Okay, you go pick up the movie while I straighten up and make a quick snack."

Barry jumped out of the bed and into the shower before going to get the movie. He hated to be funky and wouldn't dare leave the house without being so fresh and so clean. Barry stepped out of the bathroom, which was adjacent to the master bedroom, dripping wet. Pellets of water were clinging to the tiny hairs on his perfectly shaped buttocks. He flexed his biceps and gave Kelli his sexiest glare. She smiled and positioned herself on the left side of the bed.

"Dry my back, baby," he demanded and threw the towel across the room.

As Kelli rubbed his back with the towel, they both began to get aroused. Barry's skin was as smooth as a newborn baby. His dark chocolate complexion complemented his honey brown eyes. His body was well defined and he had the prettiest feet she had ever seen on a man. He kept himself well-groomed all the time. Barry was a hunk and he knew it.

Barry moved swiftly beside Kelli and began to caress her breast. He nibbled gently at her side and up to her neck, then back down to her navel. Barry lay on top without applying too much weight and slowly grinded.

CHAPTER 18

TROI

"Where's the elevator?" asked Troi.

"Elevator? I live on the second floor."

"I'm not carrying these bags up no stairs."

"Well, I'll meet you upstairs, 2b," echoed through the lobby as the stairwell door slammed with Sinclair on the other side of it. Troi impatiently pressed for the elevator, shifting her weight from one foot to the other.

Once upstairs, Troi threw her bags on the floor. "I am loving this place already," said Troi while giving the living room a once over. She walked through the dining area and into the kitchen. "Your kitchen is the bomb, girl. I wish I had this much space."

"Thanks. I had the counters done over to make more room."

Troi took a tour of the rest of the apartment before plopping down on the sofa. "I am so proud of you. You've really done well for yourself. All you need now is a good man and you'll be set." "See, Troi, there you go with that need a man shit. That's your problem. It ain't always about a man."

"I'm just saying," said Troi before being cut off by Sinclair.

"No, what are you saying? You don't need a man to complete yourself."

"Look, don't start lecturing me. I just happen to be very fond of the penis."

"What you are is a whore," said Sinclair with a smirk on her face.

"I keep telling you heifers that I ain't no whore."

"Let's eat," said Sinclair as she walked toward the kitchen. I've got Hamburger Helper, beef patties, some leftover lasagna, or I can make my famous chili tacos."

"The ones you used to make at our sleepovers at Kelli's grandma's house?"

"Yes ma'am," said Sinclair shaking her head up and down and grinning ear to ear. "Troi, remember that time we spent the night at Kelli's grandma's house so that we could go to that strip show?"

"Yeah, we could do whatever we wanted when we stayed with Kelli. Remember that time we pulled an all-nighter? The sun had come up before we made it in. I thought for sure we were in trouble, but her grandmother was still sound asleep."

"Those were the days," said Sinclair as she smiled to herself.

CHAPTER 19

KELLI

It had been a while since Kelli had seen T. T had become more and more busy since Kelli seemed more and more unavailable. Barry noticed that Kelli was slowly slipping away. It seemed they had separate agendas. They both lived their daily lives separately and only met up in the bedroom. Their nightly escapades were off the hook, then by morning they pushed past one another to get dressed. The coldness could be felt in the air.

Kelli decided to surprise T to make up for her sudden disappearance, but she was the one who got the surprise instead. Kelli pulled up to T's house. She put her hazard lights on, jumped out, and walked over to T's and rang the bell. She waited for a while, but no one answered. She recalled seeing the second-floor light on when she first pulled up, so she rang the bell again, but again no one answered. "Oh well, I tried," she mumbled to herself and jumped back into her ride.

She sat with the car in park while she searched for track twelve on her new mixed CD she had just picked up from 125th street. She let the windows down, opened her sun roof, and as she adjusted her rearview mirror, she noticed a woman approaching. The woman caught her attention because she was wearing a funky ass baby blue jumpsuit. The outfit was tight as hell and the same color as her ride. "I need something like that for the boat ride next week," Kelli said to herself. Kelli kept looking in the mirror, imagining her own jumpsuit that would be personally made for her in that same color. She smiled because she knew she would look fabulous in it.

Her smile turned to a look of bewilderment as the young woman proceeded to search her purse for her keys. Almost immediately, Kelli tensed up. Her heart dropped as the woman stopped dead smack in front of T's front door. She pulled out a keychain. Now, had it been a single key, Kelli might not have tripped. But this was a full set of keys, Pathmark card, CVS card, personalized key chain, the whole kit and caboodle.

This chick was something serious. Kelli sat there in disbelief. All this time she was being chastised by T about not spending any quality time. She saw now why the phone calls had dwindled to almost none and why T was always busy whenever she called. Kelli was pissed as hell. Then she suddenly began to laugh. She laughed to keep from crying, then laughed even harder at the fact that she had allowed herself to almost cry. "Snap out of it, girl," she said out loud.

Anyone paying her any attention would think she was crazy as she talked to herself, laughing loudly with tears in her eyes. "I am a nut," she muttered. Kelli advanced the track to sixteen and put the car in reverse, then drove and sped off with "Coming Home" from New Edition's Greatest Hits blaring from the speakers. "That's right, baby," she announced to the world, "I'm coming home." It was an old cut, but it suited the mood perfectly.

CHAPTER 20

SINCLAIR

Sinclair and Banks pulled up to the Colonial housing project. Both were excited as two little kids at Christmas. Banks was finally home and Sinclair was finally going to meet his family and see her girls. She hadn't been home in three years.

Once on the 8th floor, the elevator door opened. The hallway smelled the same as Banks remembered, like peppermint. Mrs. Henry in 8F always made it her business to keep her floor smelling good. She couldn't help how the lobby and the elevator smelled, but the 8th floor stayed on point.

Banks knocked on the door and waited in anticipation. He hadn't told anyone he was coming. The door opened.

"What's up, Cousin?" said a man about the same age as Banks but with less facial hair and build. It was Craig, Banks' cousin who he was raised with. Banks' mom had died when he was a toddler and her sister took him in as if he was her own. Craig was more like Banks' brother than cousin.

"Why didn't you let someone know you were coming?" questioned Craig as he gave his big cousin a bear hug. "What you been up to?" he said, a little annoyed that Banks had stayed away so long. "Come in, this is still your home."

Banks walked into the apartment and Sinclair followed. "Craig, this here is my lady, Sinclair."

"Nice to meet you," stated Craig.

CHAPTER 21

CAMILLE

Camille felt herself sinking into a deep depression. Her relationship with Dave was slowly changing and she couldn't figure out why. She loved him. He said he loved her, but his disappearing acts and no shows were becoming more frequent. He hardly texted her back and when he did, it was at his leisure.

She tried to keep busy with her girls and with work, but at night she really missed him.

She didn't know who to call first. Troi or Caprise. They both had their own drama going on. Troi was now about seven months pregnant and unable to locate the father and Caprise was running around ready to pounce on Joe's tenderoni.

They all were busy with their own lives. It was times like this that she was happy Sean was in her corner.

Even now, Sean still had her back. They didn't have any children together, but he still loved her and would come through if she needed help.

Camille smiled as she dialed Sean's number. "Call me when you get this message," she said into the phone.

Chapter 22

KELLI

Barry looked Kelli over as she sauntered into the living room. She dropped her keys in the bowl on the table as usual, and kicked off her shoes at the foot of the end table.

"Where are you coming from, all jazzed up?" he asked.

"Nowhere special, I just had a few errands to run."

Kelli kept replaying the scene in her head from T's house. It was over. She was done experimenting and getting hurt in the process. This was supposed to be fun.

Little did she know she was T's plaything. T enjoyed Kelli's company and she was a sucker for big breasts, but she was getting more serious with Joe. If Kelli had only known that T was actually the Toni that her good friend's husband was having an affair with, she would have never fallen the way she did. Toni had made her feel special and broke up the monotony in her own marriage, but it was only to pass the time until she could steal Joe away from Caprise. She was cutting all her playthings off one by one. Joe had finally said the words she longed to hear. "I love you." It was on her voicemail, but she heard it loud and clear.

Kelli would have been heartbroken if she knew she was being played from the get go, but she had no clue. Lucky for her, she saw it with her own eyes and realized she had a good man at home. Barry was none the wiser about her several escapades with T.

Chapter 23

TROI

Troi was running late to her own baby shower. She was always late to every function, whether it was her own or someone else's event.

Her girls had spent the previous evening setting up the Hall. The theme was pretty in pink since she was having a girl. Troi was happy with the name she had chosen, Jayden Skye.

Her biggest concern was what to wear. She had four outfits to choose from. The peach sundress made her skin glow, but it made her breasts sit too high. The cream dress was a little too formal. It was her baby shower, but not her wedding. She decided on the mint green jumpsuit which matched the décor of the room. It complemented her skin tone, form fitting, but not too tight on her medium frame and it didn't make her breasts sit up under her chin. She had packed on the pregnancy thirty in all the right places.

She was in contact with Sinclair ever since the infamous announcement text. She would never forget that day as long as she lived. When the mail notification popped up on her phone, she had no idea that it would change her life forever. The pic had the caption, "I said yes" and then the photo was her best friend and a man that she didn't know well, but who she'd had a wild night with several months ago. He was the last man that she had been with and the father of her unborn child. She sat alone in her apartment, dazed and unsure of what to do first. How was this going to play out? How was Sinclair going to take the news?

Chapter 24

CAPRISE

"Sinclair, Joe is leaving me. He asked for a divorce last night."

"Are you serious?" asked Sinclair.

"He is leaving me for that bitch!" Caprise yelled into her cell. "After all these years, I put up with his shit."

Sinclair sat on the other end of the phone, stunned. Caprise had put up with a lot over the years. Several years ago, Joe was laid off after a work injury and had gotten addicted to pain medication. He then started drinking and sunk to an all-time low. Caprise stuck with him and helped him get his life back in order. She took on three jobs to support them and never complained.

Chapter 25

Camille

Camille's phone began to vibrate on the marble countertop. She looked at the screen and Sean's face stared back at her. It was a picture of him that she took a few years ago while they vacationed in Puerto Rico. He had on a white, button down, linen shirt with the sleeves rolled up to his elbows and khaki shorts.

That trip was amazing. They had conquered a hike in the rain forest El Younque and experienced zip lining for the first time together.

"Hello?"

Camille was hesitant, but she decided to open up to Sean. "I just wanted to hear your voice."

"Oh, that's nice. You miss me, huh?"

Camille could hear him smirking through the phone. She smiled, feeling a little embarrassed but not ashamed. "We should have brunch one afternoon."

"We should," he said. "Set it up."

"Okay, I will. We can talk more then," she responded. "Talk to you soon."

Chapter 26

KELLI

Kelli and Barry's marriage was finally heating up. Being played by another woman had opened Kelli's eyes. No one would or could love her like Barry. It was rocky for a while, but she deserved better than what Toni was giving.

Barry was a good guy at heart. He didn't deserve being lied to by Kelli. All he wanted to do was make her happy, but it seemed like she needed much more. If she didn't straighten up and fly right, she was going to lose the best thing that ever happened to her.

Toni finally came clean with Kelli and explained that she had been seeing a guy over time. She apologized profusely, telling her that she didn't mean to lead her on. She was caught up while waiting to see if this relationship she was in was going anywhere. The guy she was involved with was in the process of divorcing his wife, but she wasn't totally convinced. Turns out he was telling the truth and the papers were finally filed. He moved out of the marital home and invited Toni to move in. It was real and so she had to let Kelli go.

Kelli didn't appreciate the way Toni went about it, but deep down she thanked God for the detour. Had Toni not played her, she would not be on her way back from D.R. with the love of her life. Seven days in heaven with Barry cured her temporary state of confusion and hurt. It was indeed the best vacation of her life. It was almost guaranteed that she would never experience that with Toni and so it was best that they parted ways.

Chapter 27

Caprise

Caprise pulled her five piece luggage out of the guest room closet. She filled one with her designer shoes and purses. She was fearful that Joe would destroy some of her things just like he was destroying their marriage. The others, she filled with work outfits and weekend outfits. She couldn't take it all, but she had no desire to come back at least for a few weeks. She needed to find an apartment. In the meantime, she would call Sinclair to see if she could hang out there for a while.

She hadn't seen Sinclair in a good while and wanted to get the full story on the situation with her and Troi. Sinclair had only been dating for a few months before her boo popped the question. They were at an amusement park in Philly. After a day of thrilling rides and funnel cake, he took her on the Ferris wheel. At first, Sinclair was reluctant because even though she got on some of the scariest roller coasters, they were quick, but the Ferris wheel moved slowly

177

and she was really afraid of heights. He told her to close her eyes as the cart ascended. Once at the top, he took out the small box and told her to open her eyes.

Sinclair was in shock. They had only been dating for approximately five and a half months, but she knew that he was the man of her dreams.

She immediately said yes and snapped a picture of the two of them at the top of the Ferris wheel. She couldn't even wait to get to the bottom before she sent the text to all the girls with the caption, "I said yes."

Chapter 28

SINCLAIR

"I can't believe how fast time is flying. I'm getting married in a few months and Troi's baby shower is today. What a year it has been."

"Yes, what a year," Caprise agreed. "I'm single again after ten years of marriage, Camille is back with her first love Sean, Joe is shacking up with Kelli's side piece. Who would have thought?" Both ladies burst into laughter. "I truly didn't think we'd get to this point in our lives. We almost lost thirty years of friendship over poor decisions.

When Caprise finally confided in her girlfriends about her deteriorating marriage, it was like a volcanic explosion. Turns out Kelli's dip in the lady pond was with the pretty young thing that Joe had confessed his love for. It was not pretty when it was going down. Time had partially healed their wounds.

"I'll tell you like this...I believe it was God's plan. I love Troi like a sister. It was hard to swallow at first, but it was just a coincidence. We had no idea that my Banks and her Kyle were one and the same. They had a one night stand. Even though I will always be reminded of their history by Jaydan Skye, I'm so in love with my King and I think we have a great future ahead of us. He has always been honest with me and I accept our situation. If I can accept him, why wouldn't I continue to love Troi like a sister?"

"I guess," said Caprise. "I owe Toni a beat down on sight. Kelli won't divulge any info on that skank because she doesn't want to blow up her spot with Barry. He has no clue about Toni or T, whatever her name is. He thinks she was messing around with some dude name Tony. I'm going to let her live though because Joe and I were bound to be over sooner or later. She and Barry have a chance at forever. My lips will forever be sealed."

"It's time to break barriers, sis," Sinclair continued. "We have to stop blocking our blessings. Yes, you're single now, but you're happier than I've ever seen you before. I see you traveling the world like a rock star. I'm surprised you're even in town for the shower."

"Are you kidding me? I wouldn't miss this for the world. And I'll be back for your wedding too. I wish I could have been a bridesmaid. The ladies are going to look beautiful."

Chapter 29

Camille

Camille and Sean sat and talked for hours after finishing their meal. She caught him up on what was happening with the girls. He was especially taken aback by the news of Troi and Sinclair's ordeal. It was the elephant in the room amongst the girls. Troi and Sinclair were good so far, but everyone else wasn't convinced that everything would be so good once the baby arrived.

"So, Camille, what's up with you? More importantly what's up with us?"

"We cool," Camille replied.

"I know we cool. What I want to know is what's up with us? I'm growing tired of waiting for you to stop playing games. You know that dude was no good for you. Now that you see I only have the best interest for you, are you ready to be mine again?"

Camille was smiling on the inside, but she didn't want to show it. Sean was absolutely the best thing to ever happen to her. The past year with Dave had been plagued with turmoil. She was free now from all the drama and ready to start anew with Sean.

Chapter 30

In less than 24 hours, Sinclair, Troi, Kelli, Caprise and Camille would be all together again in the same room. They had been friends for over twenty-five years and never imagined just how connected they really were.

To be continued...

www.ingramcontent.com/pod-product-compliance
Lightning Source LLC
Chambersburg PA
CBHW071312200626
46813CB00015B/1584